Death Comes to Redhawk

Books by R.G. Yoho

Kellen Malone Series
Death Comes to Redhawk

Coming Soon!
Death Rides the Rail
Nightfall Over Nicodemus
The Evil Day
Palo Duro
Long Ride to Yesterday
Boot Hill Valley
Return to Matewan
America's History is His Story

For more information
visit: www.SpeakingVolumes.us

Death Comes to Redhawk

R.G. Yoho

SPEAKING VOLUMES, LLC
NAPLES, FLORIDA
2021

Death Comes to Redhawk

Cover design by Hannah Linder

ISBN 978-1-64540-646-4

I wish to dedicate this book to Dad. I miss you.

Chapter One

The night was a sleeping child, peaceful, serene, but loaded with the promise of a loud awakening and needful of attention when it did.

The broad-shouldered man slept peacefully, his head resting on his saddlebags. It was the first truly restful sleep Kellen Malone had known in years, on this his first night outside Yuma Territorial Prison. Seven long years of sweat and toil were now behind him, leaving only calloused hands, a scar-covered back, and his precious dreams of revenge.

Malone had spent thirty-five years in life's schoolroom and experience had clearly been a stern teacher. The hopes he once shared with Alice Malone were now as faded as the jeans he wore; his chaps were as battered as Malone's hope for the future.

His face was burned dark from breaking rocks in the relentless, Arizona sun, and from the Indian blood that coursed through his veins. His mother had been a full-blooded Cherokee, his father a white trapper who took her away from the reservation. She survived the cruelties of the white man's government, but died giving birth to her son.

The unmistakable sound of a drawn-back pistol hammer broke the stillness of the desert morning. Malone's brown eyes were instantly alert and he cursed himself for sleeping so soundly. Instinctively, Malone's hand moved towards his gun.

"I wouldn't do that, Malone!"

Dotson was one of the guards at the prison, a cruel, sadistic man who enjoyed beating prisoners the way a fisherman enjoys tossing lines in the water. He was a lean man of average build, with wolfish eyes that twinkled brightly whenever he had the upper hand.

Dotson's eyes twinkled now.

Malone eased his hand away from the gun. "You don't mind if I get up...do you, Dotson? Wouldn't want folks thinking I died in my sleep."

"You're a sound sleeper, Malone. Might be the death of you yet," he said, grinning wickedly. "Go ahead. Get up. See if I care. You'll be spending all your here-ons laying down, anyway."

"You're getting better at slipping up on a body, Dotson."

Malone stood to his feet, knowing he could draw faster while upright. "Must be those Indian trackers back at the prison. Maybe they're rubbing off on you."

Dotson seemed to sense what Kellen was thinking. "And don't you try anything foolish, Malone! Just as soon kill you now as later."

"How'd you find me, Dotson? You couldn't track a five-legged pack mule if the critter left droppings every ten feet."

Dotson bristled at the remark. "Wasn't hard to find you, Malone. Anyone could figure you're on your way back to Redhawk to find your son."

Malone was not a fool; he had no doubt as to what Dotson had in store for him. He could only stall for time and hope for an opportunity.

"What do you want with me, Dotson?"

"Didn't think I'd let you go without saying my good-byes," he grinned, still leveling his gun at Malone's midsection. "That time you tried to escape, we had an awful time catching you."

Malone laughed out loud. "Yea, but it took you three days. Without those Apache trackers, you'd still be stumbling around in the desert, Dotson. Of course, I would probably have you by now."

"When we got you back to the prison, I'd have laid you open with that whip. That darned Ingalls had to take your side! Lost my job over the whole affair. The man's too easy on the prisoners, I think."

"Especially me?"

"Yeah! Especially you, Malone! Old George Thurlow would have given you forty lashes for an escape. Ingalls don't have the guts for the job. Didn't even add extry time to your sentence."

"Wish you had that whip with you now, Dotson. I'd feed it to you."

Dotson arrogantly threw back his head in laughter. "You seem to be forgetting something, Malone," he said, lifting the muzzle to emphasize his point. "I'm holding the six-shooter."

Malone's eyes turned cold. "You going to fire that gun or just point it at me all day?"

"What's your hurry, Malone?"

"I'm just getting sick of listening to your mouth."

"Why you filthy...!" His finger began to tense on the trigger.

"I wouldn't do that!"

"And why not?"

"You took a big chance in following me. The Apaches nearly got me yesterday. If you shoot me, every brave in earshot will come running." It was now Malone's turn to grin. "Fire that gun and you'll lose your hair."

Uncertainty showed in Dotson's eyes. "There's no Injuns around here, Malone. Who're you trying to kid?"

Kell continued to deal the cards while the game was still fresh in Dotson's mind. "You ever see a man after the Apaches got done with him? Horrible sight! Almost lost my dinner the first time I saw it.

"Apaches are experts at torture and mutilation, Dotson. They glory in it. I knew a man one time who escaped from them. He saw his friend tortured right before his eyes. Must have been having so much fun, they forgot all about him. Anyway, he told me that he heard his friend praying for death before they got done with him."

Bewildered, Dotson studied Kell's face. "You're just pulling my leg, Malone. Hoping to scare me."

Malone shook his head. "I never kid about Apaches, Dotson. I've seen some of their work. Squaws are the worst."

Dotson began to grin and shake his head. "I ain't listening to no more of your drivel. I came here to kill you and I plan to do just that.

"You remember Clay Adkins? He paid me to kill you. The fool! I'd have done it for nothing. Now nobody but the buzzards will know what happened to you."

Malone knew his bluff had been taken about as far as it would go. This hand of poker was nearly over. Dotson was going to kill him here and now, so Kell knew he must make his play. There was no decision to be made. Age and instinct had already fashioned his reactions to moments such as these. He only hoped he was still fast enough.

"Goodbye, Malone. See you in hell..."

Bracing for a bullet, Kell's hands swept down for his guns. Suddenly he heard a swishing sound, followed by a low thud. His guns came level, but no bullet came his way. Kell saw Dotson begin to sway on his feet, a queer look of disbelief in his eyes. His eyes rolled back in his head and he pitched forward on his face.

Kell could see the arrow lodged between Dotson's shoulder blades. He dove behind a rock for cover, as several more arrows split the air where he'd just been.

Breathing a sigh of relief, Kell looked over at the body of the dead guard. He could find no grief. "Hell, huh? You keep a spot warm for me, Dotson."

Stealing a quick peek from behind the rock, Malone scrambled after his rifle and canteen. He counted at least twelve Chiricahua warriors. The sight brought a profane oath to his lips. "Kellen Malone, you really got yourself into a dandy scrape this time."

***

Two weeks before Kellen Malone was to be released from prison, a tall, smartly dressed gentleman was leisurely nursing a brandy in the Lady Luck saloon. Disinterested, the richest man in Redhawk surveyed the other patrons the way a rancher might look over his herd. His gaze fell on the bartender and was met with one of disdain. Their eyes held for a minute. Clay Adkins looked away first; the bartender grunted and returned to his work.

Although friendly in casual conversation, there was an air about Clay that caused other men to avoid him. The local women found his quiet manner, if not his wealth, particularly appealing. Usually accompanied by a pair of bodyguards, no one dared to speak unkindly to Adkins since his arrival in Redhawk, no one but Kellen Malone and the burly bartender, Buck Halstead.

He motioned at Halstead, who looked disgusted but finally made his way over to Clay's table with another glass of brandy.

The bartender rudely placed, or more precisely, thrust the glass in front of him. It splashed brandy on the table and spotted Clay's finely tailored suit.

"Excuse me for being so clumsy," Halstead said sarcastically. "Don't you have somewhere to go, Clay?"

Adkins removed a handkerchief from his pocket and wiped the liquor from his clothes. "Not at the moment, Mr. Halstead. But thank you for asking."

"You know your business isn't wanted around here?"

"Yes, I know, but this is the only saloon in town."

Buck wiped his hands on his apron. "Why don't you buy one, Clay? You've bought everything else...and everybody."

"You don't think I should be ashamed of the opportunities which wealth has proffered me...do you, Mr. Halstead? And since you brought up the subject, my offer still stands for the Lady Luck. You'd be welcomed to stay on as bartender, at a quite substantial salary, I might add."

"Do you remember what I told you the last time, Clay?"

"Now let me see," Adkins said, feigning a momentary memory loss. "It seems that you said something involving the south end of a northbound donkey. Am I correct?"

"Yea, that was it, Clay." Halstead turned to go. After another look of contempt, he added, "My offer still stands there too."

Smiling, Adkins watched Halstead return to his place behind the bar. He enjoyed these conversations with the bartender, the way a cat might enjoy amusing itself with a rat when captured.

Clay sipped at his drink and recalled the attractive woman at the diner who was soon to be his wife. Mingled with his thoughts of Rachel, he considered the ranch, ten thousand beautiful acres that would soon be his. He smiled to himself, a smug look of self-satisfaction. Thus far, his plans had worked to perfection. It would only be a short time now, a matter of weeks until he would have it all. Clay gently lifted his glass, in a silent toast to his success.

Just then, the saloon doors swung open as a young freckle-faced boy burst into the room. Ordinarily, a boy entering a saloon would be greeted with icy stares, followed by a severe scolding, but not young Tommy Cline.

Tommy routinely delivered messages to the saloon's customers from the stage office. The boy was always courteous, dependable, and generally wasted no time in finding the letter's owner.

"Mr. Adkins, this letter just came on the stage for you, sir."

"Thank you, Tommy," Clay said, smiling. He gave the boy a dollar in change, an unusually large tip for any child.

Wide-eyed, Tommy looked at the money. "Is this all for me?"

"Yes, son. Take the money and run along. This is no kind of place for a youngster."

"Thank you, sir," the boy replied, happily jingling his newfound wealth as he skipped out the door.

Clay watched the boy leave, remembering the days when he too had been a child. He thought of the poverty his family had known and how much a dollar would have meant to him back then. A smile came to his face, knowing he'd brightened one day of a boy's childhood.

Adkins ripped open the letter and saw it was from Dotson. Halfway down the page he stopped, stunned and speechless. Cursing under his breath, Adkins continued. He read the note again, as if that would change the letter's original message. "Not now!" he fumed, striking his fist on the table.

At the sound of Clay's tirade, all heads in the room turned in his direction. The room grew quiet, all eyes fixed on him. They lingered for a time before returning to their drinks and various amusements.

Adkins, realizing how foolish he'd nearly been, whispered under his breath."I'm so close to having it all. I won't let Malone ruin my plans." Then he brooded silently for a few moments.

Although Clay had tried to plan for any eventuality, Malone's release was an outcome he hadn't foreseen. Knowing the sort of man Malone might be, he had always expected him to escape from Yuma Prison.

From there, it would only be a question of what would kill him first, the desert or the guards.

Dotson had been paid well for his services and personally guaranteed Malone wouldn't live out his sentence. What had gone wrong? And then he remembered Superintendent Ingalls...he was responsible. It had to be! Clay cursed the man silently. Frank Ingalls had a harsh streak to him but he was fair, a man of integrity who couldn't be bought. Adkins knew the type; he understood them none at all.

So Malone is going to be released. No matter, Clay thought. There is always Clements. The idea brought a smile to his face. He would send a telegram to Skull Clements. He would send it today.

Clay rose from his chair and tossed some money on the table to pay for his drinks. The bartender shot him a hard look, but his frown was met with a smile.

"If you change your mind, Halstead, you know where to find me."

"Yea, I know. Under some slimy rock." Halstead swallowed hard, but choked back his pride long enough to ask a question. "How's Jesse?"

"He's doing well. I'll tell him you asked."

"Thank you," Halstead muttered, the words almost catching in his throat. "You know you shouldn't have him, don't you?"

The man's eyes twinkled before he spoke. "But I do."

Halstead could think of nothing further to say and hung his head. Adkins pushed his way through the batwing doors. Enjoying the warmth of the sun, he stood on the boardwalk, reflecting on what must be done. Clements would handle things just fine. He always had in the past. Adkins immediately started towards the telegraph office.

A buckboard rumbled down the street. Clay stepped aside, waiting for it to pass. He saw the boy Tommy was in it.

"Hi, Mr. Adkins," the boy hollered, happily sucking on a peppermint stick.

He waved at the youngster. "Hello there, Tommy," Clay he said with a smile, before continuing on his way.

Clements had done some work for Adkins before and Clay always knew him to be especially tight-lipped. It was an important quality for men in Skull's line of work. The man never came cheap, Clay thought, but then quality never does. It would take him a couple of weeks to get to Redhawk, but Adkins thought it would still be in plenty of time.

"No one will mess up my plans," Clay muttered softly. "Not even Kellen Malone." He stopped outside the telegraph office door. And Dotson, Clay reflected. It was his mess; he should try to clean it up. Adkins went inside, planning to send an additional wire.

***

Malone took another careful look around, taking note of each detail, the rocks, shadows, and terrain. He had learned to do such things as a matter of habit, seldom considering his reasons for them. A man traveling though wild country must learn to be observant of every detail, for death could hinge on the one missed.

It had been some time since he had seen any Apaches, but he was not surprised. He had known some tough and seasoned cavalry officers who fought them all day and never saw a single Indian.

The sun had just begun to sneak over the mountaintops, casting eerie shadows on the jagged rocks, boulders, and vegetation around him. Each object was transformed into some kind of evil form. A nearby cholla took the shape and dimensions of a hideous monster, something ominous and frightful. With the advent of daybreak, these once-dreadful objects would always return to their normal appearance.

Kell quickly stole another look around the boulder, looking from the other side this time, trying to set no recognizable pattern. He gave careful study to everything around him. There was nothing to be seen, just the same rocks and shadows.

Shadows!

Realization came to him in a split second. Before, two rocks cast shadows next to the prickly cholla. Now there were three. The third shadow was moving slightly, slowly. Kell recognized the shape of an Apache brave.

He hurtled himself out of the way, still holding the rifle and canteen. An arrow split the air where he'd just been. Malone ran towards another rock for cover. Rifles bellowed all around him, bullets kicking dust in his face and stinging him with fragments.

Kell paused to catch his breath, knowing he'd only missed death by a heartbeat. It was a sobering thought. The Apaches had taken him for granted once; they would be more careful next time.

Kell thought himself fortunate that they hadn't hit his canteen. Indians have a vicious sense of humor and that is normally one of their first targets. He knew he had enough ammunition to stand them off for awhile if he made good use of his shots. There was water enough for a couple of days, but right then, tomorrow was the farthest thing from his mind. Kell wouldn't have laid two bits on his odds of living until nightfall.

About fifty feet ahead of him was the Indian who shot the arrow. The last time, he came out of the right side of the rock. He was still hiding there. On a hunch, Kell drew down on the left side of the rock, hoping he'd try something different next time. His Winchester was trained at belt level on a standing man, just about right for a crouching Chiricahua. He waited...

The Apache didn't disappoint him. He slipped out on the left side of the rock, just as Kell touched off a shot. He heard him yelp, and saw the brave clutching at his chest. Malone marked it down as being one less. He doubted it would make any difference.

No sooner than he dropped the warrior, three rifles barked nearly as one. Their slugs struck the rock where he was hidden, burning his eyes with sand and fragments. He rubbed them quickly until his vision returned. Kell knew they would be wary of him now, surprise no longer on their side and knowing he was a good shot.

Time passed...

Malone had to give the Apaches credit; they were patient and smart. Several times he had seen them move, and he shot, none of them scoring. He now realized he would have to be more patient, more like them. That would be his only chance in getting out of there alive. It soon paid off.

Passing up several of their attempts to draw his fire, Malone took aim where one of the Apaches had ducked under cover. Nothing moved but Kell waited. Finally he moved, just as Kell took up slack in the trigger. The Winchester jumped in his hands. He saw the Indian go down, wounded not dead. The others would come to get him soon, and Kell hoped the wounded brave would be a burden to them.

As the Chiricahua lay there hurting, Malone thought about putting another slug into him. The idea came again; it passed unheeded.

The sun had climbed high in the sky, several hours passing since the first attack. Heat waves shimmered and danced in the distance. Kell reloaded, checked his six-guns, and took a long pull from his canteen. He looked again and saw nothing. They were in no hurry. It was a quality the Apache had mastered.

Sweat trickled down his back. His clothes smelled of dust, stale sweat, and gunpowder. Malone leaned against one rock, while hiding behind another. It felt cool against his back. He thought of water once again, his canteen still over half full. It would have to last him.

Checking his horse with a quick glance, Kell saw the animal was still all right. "How are you doing, fellow?" he said gently.

He doubted that the animal understood, but talking made him feel better. No one could sneak up behind them, because he'd made camp against a sheer rock wall, towering two hundred feet high. Their only means of attack must come from the front. Then he remembered the wall. The Apaches might go around the mountain, shooting their rifles down at him from the top of the bluff. It was something he would keep in mind.

Kell peered around the rock quickly, trying to discover their game this time. They were not anywhere in sight, and it was quiet. Kell didn't like it one bit.

Then it started...

Malone fired his twin guns fast as he could work them, burning at least one of the braves. They kept coming as his guns emptied and he levered his rifle furiously.

Suddenly, as if they came forth right out of the dust, four of them were upon him. There was no time for thought, just action. Kell blasted one of them at point blank range with his rifle. Its heavy slug knocked him backward, stone-cold dead. He triggered it again at the other brave. Nothing!

He stepped in quickly, slashing at Kell with a knife. It split his shirt and left a bloody stripe across his chest. As he came in for another, Malone clubbed him alongside the skull with his Winchester, crushing the Indian's skull just behind his ear.

The third one tried to run him through with a lance. Kell caught the weapon in the crook of his arm, pulling the brave forward. Then he put a big foot in the Indian's chest, violently kicking him into the dust.

A bullet from outside the camp burned his shoulder, causing him to drop the lance. Malone pulled his boot knife and flung it at the brave as he tried to get up. It buried itself to the hilt in his throat. He made a hoarse, choking sound as he struggled to get up, then lay still.

The last warrior was the biggest of the three, a man wiry and strong. Kell met him coming in with a hard right hand. He smiled through bloody lips, as he lunged with a knife. Malone ducked under his charge, caught the arm with both hands, turning his body as he grabbed him. All in one motion, he flipped the Indian over his shoulder into the dust.

The brave scrambled to his feet quickly, easily. Fighting was a way of life to his people and Apaches became skilled in its art from childhood. This man was probably a great warrior among his people, Kell thought. They circled each other warily, Malone without a weapon. Faster than a rattler strikes at its victim, the knife slashed and darted at Kell. So far, Malone had been able to elude the attacks. He knew it was more luck than skill.

When he slashed at Kell again, Malone caught his wrist and they both went to the ground. Going down, Kell's head hit a rock and he could feel a wave of darkness and nausea sweeping over him. To lose consciousness was to die, so he fought that also.

Rolling over and over in the dust, he struggled to keep the Indian's blade away from his throat. The Apache straddled him there on the ground, the knife only inches away. For what seemed like an hour to Kell, they stayed like that, the life of one dependent on the death of the other. Battle-weary, sweat pouring off of him, and his throat parched from thirst, Kell almost gave up the fight.

Then calling on his last reserves of strength, he grunted hard and pushed the knife away. Kell hammered his ear with a right, again and again. Once more, they rolled across the ground, this time with Malone coming out on top. The will to live being greater than his thirst or exhaustion, he turned the Chiricahua's wrist, plunging the blade deep into his chest. Still, the Apache continued to struggle...

While still holding on to him, Kell grabbed the brave's black hair with his other hand. Filled with only a lust to kill, to survive, he pounded his head up and down against a rock. How many times, he didn't know. The Apache's dark eyes closed; the struggle ceased; his body lay still. Only then did he stop.

Gasping for air, Malone crawled away from the body. He came to his feet, and then fell down again from weakness. Hearing moccasins shift on the sand, he turned his head...

Coming his way, there was the warrior Kell thought he had killed. His head and chest were covered with blood, yet somehow he had wrenched the knife from his chest. A walking dead man still clutching the knife, the brave staggered towards Malone.

Kell tried to roll away from the attack, his outstretched arm finding the other Indian's lance. Game till the end, the Apache gave a war cry, diving for the final kill. Malone brought the lance up to meet his attack. It struck the Indian squarely in the chest, impaling him. He grunted hard as Kell gave the lance a hard, upward thrust. With that, the Chiricahua, finally dead, pitched over on the ground beside Malone.

Kell quickly located his guns, punched out the empties, and immediately reloaded. All around him, the ground was littered with bodies.

His breath coming in painful gasps, he leaned back against the rock, and checked his wounds. A bullet had just creased the fleshy part of his shoulder. The wound looked and felt a lot worse than it really was. Kell figured he'd probably live...the thought made him laugh.

Malone's throat was dry. He touched his lips and felt they were growing parched and brittle. He cursed when he located his canteen. Sometime during the battle, a bullet or a ricochet had stuck the canteen, draining most of it. Craning his neck back as far as it would go, he downed the last swallow remaining in his canteen. He held it on his tongue, savoring the cool, sweetness of it. Before taking the final swallow down his throat, he swished it from side to side in his mouth. He wanted to remember its taste.

Hours passed...

Stealing another look, Kell saw that the first two Indians he shot had been dragged away. It didn't surprise him, for their people rarely leave a body, dead or alive, to lie where it had fallen. For that reason alone, a man never knew how many Indians he had actually killed. The number is usually less than a man might think. These other four bodies they would get later, as soon as Kell left, or as soon as he was dead.

Malone knew it wouldn't be long until they rushed him again. There looked to be twelve to fifteen of them earlier. He'd killed five and wounded two more. That didn't even the odds too much. It would be nightfall in a couple of hours and he knew many of the tribes wouldn't fight after dark.

Some Apaches were afraid if they were killed at night, their spirits would wander forever in darkness. Kell wasn't going to bet his life on it. Some of them might not know about the superstitions. The younger braves, often foolish, might not care.

After dark, Kell knew that was the time he must try to escape. Somehow, he knew he must make it through their midst, unseen. It would not be easy, but it was possible.

At the Alamo, George Webb Slaughter, carrying messages, scaled the walls, and passed through the Mexican lines several times. But these were not Mexicans; these were Apaches, hardly the same thing. No matter, he thought. Malone's wells of patience were as dry as his canteen. Come nightfall, he knew he must try.

The sun continued its brutal assault as the heat began to play tricks on his mind. For a moment, he found himself back at the ranch, drinking from the mountain spring. The water flowed from a crevice in the rocks, in a place known only to Kell and Jesse.

The cattle on his range never went thirsty, a fact that led to questions, curiosity, and a great deal of speculation among the other ranchers. Kell had often supplied many of them with water, bringing it down from the mountain by the wagonload. Even during the driest of months, the spring continued to run freely; cold, clear and fresh. He could almost taste it now, but reality soon interrupted his thoughts.

Malone's neck twitched and he had the feeling he was being watched, studied. It was the same feeling a man gets when he thinks someone is staring at him and he turns to look, only to find himself staring the watcher directly in the eye. Kell suddenly had that feeling. While squatting on his heels, he turned his head suddenly...

Standing there on the cliff, with a rifle trained down on him, he saw another Apache. Throwing his body to one side, he managed to escape a killing shot from above.

The slug had been right on target, but instinct saved his life once again.

Crouching next to an overhanging rock, one that offered some shelter from above, he tried to locate a target on the bluff. Kell could see nothing.

Now that they had him surrounded, it could only mean one thing. They would be coming soon, all of them.

Malone could feel it.

Chapter Two

The desert is a harsh and brutal place, yet beautiful in its rugged terrain. There are dozens of ways to die in the desert so nothing must be taken for granted. Those who fear the desert never see the beauty; those who see only the beauty never learn to fear. Those who see both may often survive.

A kingdom ruled by the iron hand of nature, the desert is no place for the meek of heart. It offers no preeminence to social standing or earthly title. Those who come within its borders are bound by only two rules: the weak are taken and the strong survive. That is the nature of the desert, as it often is with man.

Kellen Malone knew those rules and accepted them. This knowledge made his survival no less difficult, yet it fully prepared him to face one of the desert's greatest dangers, the Apache.

With some measure of regret, Malone figured that his time for this world was growing short. He could hear them moving closer. Kell counted his cartridges and found he had plenty. He didn't bother counting the odds; they were not in his favor, anyway.

The Chiricahuas had begun to show themselves more often, every sighting a grim reminder that the noose was being drawn tighter and tighter around his neck.

A man really only fears death when he has some good reason to live. After Alice died, many had been the time Kell wished he could join her. But now he remembered Jesse. His son would be fourteen now and needful of a man's guidance. Longingly, Kell thought of Jesse and knew he wanted to live.

The air grew quiet and Malone could sense that something was about to happen. He peered around the rock and cursed bitterly when he saw them.

"Here they come," he muttered. Kell began to fire, choosing his targets with care. "Come and get it, doggone you! Come on!" He dusted one of the Apache warriors.

Then, as suddenly as the attack had begun, it ceased. Malone was bewildered but thankful.

Suddenly he heard the sound of fast-approaching hoofbeats. Then he saw a rider, a white man, hunkered down low in the saddle. Malone figured that the heat must have been getting to him again. His gnawing thirst and delirious eyes and ears both were playing tricks on him. Kell blinked again, but there he was.

An Indian suddenly loomed ahead of the rider. The horseman, still at full gallop, snapped off a shot. The Apache was slammed to the ground as the slug found its mark.

"That was fine shooting," Malone muttered underneath his breath.

As the rider drew nearer, Kell stole another look above. The Indian on the bluff had a rifle trained on the unsuspecting stranger. Leaping out into the open, Malone triggered his Winchester on the Indian above.

It was a quick shot, and for just a brief moment, Malone thought he'd missed. The Apache, seemingly unharmed, stood there for a time, rifle still in hand. He staggered stupidly, before pitching forward. The Indian fell two hundred feet to the rocks below, the impact finishing the job the slug left undone. His body struck the earth violently, with a gut-wrenching, sickening thud, which could be heard from twenty feet away.

In spite of the circumstances, the stranger could be seen smiling as he leaped his horse into the area where Malone made camp. Dismounting quickly, he left the animal ground hitched. Keeping his head low and carrying a long gun, he sprinted for the precious cover of the rocks. A canteen was slung over his shoulder. Bullets kicked dust all around him.

As he came closer, Kell appraised the man carefully. He wore black jeans, covered with miles of trail dust and alkali. His recently-cleaned shirt was stained with sweat. Leaning his rifle alongside the rock, he sat down beside Malone. The stranger gave a nod in the direction of the Apaches. "Friends of yours?"

"Not yet," Malone grinned. "But we've spent several hours trying to get close." With a look of envy, he took note of the canteen the man was carrying.

"You got any water to spare? Indians got mine earlier. Left me with a bad case of cotton mouth."

"Yeah, I got plenty. Help yourself." Ignoring the Indians as if they weren't there, he reached into his vest pocket, took out his makings, and proceeded to roll a smoke. "Want some?"

"No, I'll pass. Those Apaches are still out there," Malone explained. "I'd like to keep my hands free."

"Suit yourself, friend. I reckon you held 'em off this long. Couple of more minutes won't matter none. A man don't get much chance to smoke while riding through wild country," he observed. The stranger did not lift his eyes, still preoccupied with the task at hand.

"Yeah," Kell said. "The glow of a cigarette makes a good mark to shoot at."

As the man lit the cigarette, his eyes lifted. He smiled at Kell then. "Reckon I owe you one, friend. That Injun on the bluff would have fetched me for sure. Thanks!"

"It was my pleasure," Malone said, offering his hand. "He nearly got me a while earlier."

The stranger stopped to shake his hand. He looked at the bandage on Kell's arm, then at the blood and dead bodies Indians around him.

"Looks like you had a bad time here, mister. From the looks of things, they got the worst of it. Notice you ain't scalped none of 'em yet. What're you waiting for?"

"They were good fighters. All of them died game...especially that one," Malone replied, pointing at the one he'd run through with a lance. "Almost killed me after he was dead."

"Still ain't answered my question yet.

"Even an Apache won't mutilate a dead man who fought well. So why should I? Besides, there's another reason."

"What's that?"

"I don't have any use for a man who goes around lifting hair, mine or anyone else's." Malone's eyes turned cold. "You got a problem with that?"

"No, I don't." Smugly, the stranger took a long pull at his cigarette. "I feel the same way you do. Just wanted to read the brand you were wearing. Always like to know who I'm sharing a camp with."

Malone saw an Indian trying to sneak towards them. He snapped off a shot, but the Chiricahua ducked just in time.

"You get him?"

"No, but it ought to keep him honest."

The stranger turned the bodies over with his foot." Looks like he swallowed something that didn't agree with him," he smiled, nodding at the one killed with the lance. Grabbing the dead warrior by the hair, he lifted the face for a closer look.

"Well, I'll be cussed! Do you know who this is?"

"Probably the toughest fighting man I ever faced," Malone grinned. "I hope he doesn't have any brothers. If they came gunning for me, I'd just kill myself and save them the trouble."

"This here is Running Hawk, one of the meanest renegade Apaches in the territory. They say he's been running with Geronimo. They've been killing and looting all over the place, clear into Mexico."

"Geronimo? I thought he was on the reservation in San Carlos."

"Not anymore. Seems they weren't satisfied with the accommodations. Surprised you ain't heard about it. Military's been chasing them for months."

As tired as he was, Malone still managed to smile. "You don't get much news where I just came from."

"Yuma?"

Kell nodded.

"Reckon you don't." Whatever else the stranger wanted to say went unsaid.

"Last I heard, General Crook had the Apache situation under control."

"He did for a while, but Washington sent him to Nebraska. General Nelson Miles is in charge now."

"Miles?" Kell shot back. "Brave man, but he couldn't find his butt with both hands. They should have left Crook in charge. He's a good man . . . honest one too. The Indians trust him. Miles is a filthy, lying glory-hound. The man gets things done, but he's none too choosy about his methods.

"You know him too, I take it?"

"I know of him." Kell fired another shot at one of the warriors, hitting nothing but air. "Geronimo, huh? Did you know that was the name the Mexicans gave him? The Apaches call him Goyathlay. It means one who yawns."

"Well, ain't nobody yawned much since he fled the reservation. With Running Hawk dead, some of the fight will go right out of them. It'll make you a big man among the Apaches. Big medicine. Probably send all their braves to test you. A lot of men fought him; none lived to brag about it." The stranger flicked his cigarette away and grabbed his rifle. He chose a defensive position there among the rocks.

Kell slumped to the ground, nearly exhausted. "Right now, I don't feel in much of a bragging mood."

For the first time since the rider's arrival, he got a good, clear look at the man's face. The stranger had been taking great pains to hide the left side of his face, a habit long since acquired. Now Kell knew why. A look of recognition came to his eyes.

"You know me, don't you, friend?"

"Yes, I know you. You're Joe Clements."

Clements was a gunfighter, one of the best. His given name was Joe, but most folks knew him as "Skull." It had been the name that stuck, originating from the skull-shaped scar on his left cheek, earned in a brutal knife fight at a little saloon in Abilene, Texas.

"I figured you must have recognized me. With this mark of banished Cain on my cheek, it's hard to go unnoticed."

"It does kind of stand out," Kell observed, "but that isn't how I know you. We met once...before the scar, I mean."

Clements scratched his head, searching his mind for distant memories. His mind came up with nothing.

"Austin, that day you wiped out the Palance brothers."

"Well, I thought you looked familiar. You're that hombre who covered my back when the barkeep went for a shotgun. I never saw him reaching," Clements explained. "He'd have plugged me for sure if you hadn't made it your play. Shucked your gun mighty fast...fastest I ever saw. Earp, Hardin, Hickok, Candrey...they're all supposed to be good. Bet they couldn't touch you for speed."

"Some folks would throw your name in that pot, Joe. I'd be one of them, because I've seen you shoot. Those Palance boys were pretty salty customers."

"I was in fine form that day," he replied, showing a grin to go along with a slight trace of embarrassment. "Three of them, there were. I walked away without a scratch, thanks to you. I guess I owe you more than one, Malone...wasn't it?"

"That's right. Kellen Malone."

Clements noticed the other dead body nearby, with the arrow stuck in his back. "Too bad about your friend over there, Malone. Never knew what hit him...did he?"

Kell laughed out loud. "I've called that man a lot of things over the years, but friend was never one of them. His name is Dotson. Used to be one of the guards at the prison. Probably give the buzzards a sour stomach."

"Sounds like you were real close," Clements smiled.

"Let's just say none of Yuma's prisoners will mourn his passing. Least of all me."

"What happened?"

"He followed me out here, Joe. It seems Dotson took a personal interest in my welfare." Kell studied his surroundings, looking for any movement. "Had the drop on me when they killed him."

"Lucky for you."

"Doggone shame they had to kill him."

"Why do you say that, Malone?"

"Cheated me out of the pleasure." Malone took another look around. It had been a while since there had been any shooting and they had seen no movement. "Do you hear that, Joe?"

"Yeah, I surely do. Right peaceful, ain't it?"

"They must have given up. Apaches love a good scrap, but not if it costs them too many bodies."

"This one got a little expensive," Joe added. "From the amount of blood, I'd say you got at least two out beyond the camp. That's how I happened upon you. A shod horse, traveling alone—figured it had to be white man."

"Only half white."

"Don't make no difference to me. I've known some good ones in all colors. A man's heart ain't revealed by the shade of his face." Clements laughed out loud. "I'll try to ignore the fact you're a half-breed, if you'll try to forget the fact that I'm mean and ugly. Besides, I need your help getting through the territory and your gun shoots like it's all purebred."

"We'd better wait a couple of hours, just to make sure they're gone. Besides, we'll make better time after it's dark. It's cooler then too," Kell offered. "I'm on my way to Redhawk."

"Redhawk, you say?" Clements asked strangely, his eyes taking on a serious look. "Mind if I tag along?" I'm getting tired of these one-sided conversations with my horse." Clements grinned. "The animal don't really say much. Thinks he's too good to talk to me."

"Knew a man one time who had a fine horse like that one. Used to talk to it all the time, long-winded speeches that went on forever. One day the animal just ups and throws him from the saddle. Broke his neck, too."

Clements' eyes widened. "What happened, Malone? Rattlesnake spook him?"

"No," Kell replied with a grin. "The horse just wanted a little peace and quiet." He laughed before taking a long pull from the canteen. "Be glad to have the company, Joe."

"About the canteen, Malone. You keep it."

"Thanks, Joe."

"Think nothing of it. Got another one hanging on my saddle." Clements paused then and started to build another smoke. "Stranger tried to rob me about fifty miles back." He smiled as he saw the question in Kell's eyes. "He won't be needing it, Malone. The hombre won't hold no water, anyhow."

***

Twenty miles north of the Mexican border, a platoon of soldiers rested their horses from the long day's ride. Many of them, little more than youngsters, rigidly sat at attention in their saddles. Under the watchful eye of the general, no one felt at ease to relax. Occasionally, one of the troops would succumb to the heat and exhaustion, falling from the saddle of his horse. The fallen cavalryman was then given a ration of water, followed by a stern scolding. After a few minutes to recover, he was then remounted.

General Nelson A. Miles turned up his nose at the rancid smell of stale sweat that clung to his body. He rubbed his face, desperately in need of a shave. His uniform needed cleaned and pressed, Miles' once sharp creases now only a vague memory. It was no way for an officer of the U.S. Cavalry to look. The general cursed the blistering desert heat. Most of all, he cursed Geronimo.

"You Chiricahua scouts are rumored to be some of the finest trackers in the land. All I've gotten so far is talk and empty promises," Miles said, pointing a finger in the Indians' faces. "If you can't find Geronimo's camp, I'll find someone who will!"

"General!" Lieutenant Charles B. Gatewood called out, while riding back toward the soldiers. "Excuse me, Sir." He smartly executed a salute before approaching the general's horse. "The scouts say there are a couple of riders just to the west of us."

Miles returned Gatewood's salute. "Are they white men?"

"They appear to be, sir. Both of them are riding saddled horses. You want them stopped?"

"Yes, Gatewood. Take ten men with you and ascertain what their business might be. Then bring them here to me."

Gatewood snapped off his best salute and reined his horse around. He started to ride away, but the general's voice stopped him.

"And Lieutenant Gatewood, any hostile action on their part is to be met in kind. Is that clear?"

"Yes, sir!" Gatewood checked the loads in his pistol. "Quite clear."

Miles watched the lieutenant ride away after first selecting his men. Gatewood is a good soldier and brave, he thought. He wished he had a whole platoon of men like him. The general wouldn't balk at storming the gates of Hell leading a troop of Gatewoods.

Miles reined his horse around, immediately continuing his rebuke of the two Apache scouts. "If you men don't find Geronimo's camp soon, you'll find yourself on one of those trains taking the Apaches to Florida. Do you understand me?"

The Apaches nodded.

"Now get out there!" Miles fumed, as the scouts rode away. "And bring me something other than excuses!" The general swore again softly. "Now, where is that Geronimo?"

***

A man's opinion of himself and that held by others are seldom the same. Man has a tendency to think of himself, not as how he is, but rather as how he wishes to be. As Kell rode along silently, he wondered what sort of man he'd become and how much prison had changed him.

Malone always considered himself to be a good man, steady, the kind of person one could count on in a pinch. He ran short on patience and long on loyalty, to a friend or a cause. Those qualities, he believed, had not changed.

But what of prison? Some would see him as a criminal, a man whose motives would always fall under question. Malone realized he couldn't change the opinions of a scattered few. The folks who really mattered, his friends and loved ones, wouldn't accept the law's decision of his guilt. Kell decided to ride into Redhawk, head held high, and let his critics be cursed.

"You see 'em, Malone?"

"Yeah, I see them. They've been up there for a while now." Malone took a drink from his canteen. "They look like Apaches. Wonder what they're waiting for, Joe."

Malone drew the rifle from its scabbard and gently laid it across his thighs. Joe apparently thought the idea had some merit, because he did the same.

Clements shielded his eyes from the sun and stared at the hill. "Looks like we won't be long finding out. They're coming this way." His gun lifted for what was to come.

"Wait a minute, Joe. There are soldiers with them. Must be part of Miles' outfit, still hunting for Geronimo."

Malone watched as the ten soldiers and a couple of Indian scouts rode down towards them. Never known as a trusting soul, Kell kept his rifle close to hand. He held it loosely, as if its aim on Gatewood's belly was by accident. Clements had already put away his Winchester, but his hand rested lightly on his thigh, close to his six-gun.

No doubt the soldiers would take them if any shooting started, but Kellen knew they wouldn't go alone. Clements' skill with a gun was unchallenged. Undoubtedly, there would be several empty saddles when the smoke cleared.

The lieutenant rode directly up to their horses. The others fanned out around them. Malone, no stranger to the military, saw their action as a warning not to resist. Kell could feel the rage building in his soul. Like a wounded animal trapped in a corner, Malone bared his teeth whenever he felt pushed or threatened.

"Morning to you, Lieutenant," Malone offered. There was no humor hiding behind his smile.

Gatewood saw the gun pointed at his belly and immediately recognized Malone's intention for what it was. "I am Lieutenant Charles B. Gatewood, assigned to General Nelson Miles. You men are hereby ordered to throw down your weapons!"

"I don't care if your name's Ulysses S. Grant," Malone replied. "I'm not giving up my guns, to you or anyone else. And I don't like taking orders. Seven long years of it was enough."

"You will drop them, sir, or I'll be forced to take action!"

"Do as you see fit, Lieutenant. Just so you know you'll be the first one to die." Malone's eyes turned cold. "If you so much as move a muscle, I'll blast you out of that saddle. Probably get a couple more before I go down."

"Malone," Clements added, "I'll leave the big-nosed lieutenant to you. But I got ten dollars that says I can empty three more of them saddles before they take me."

Lieutenant Gatewood liked nothing about his present situation. Although he knew that their superior numbers would ultimately allow them to prevail against the two strangers, the young military officer also knew he would not be alive to see it. Despite his youth, he had lived long enough to recognize that men such as these were not simply making vain threats. The men in front of him had killed before. And if necessary, they would do so again.

"What can we do for you, Lieutenant?"

"General Miles has been given the duty of the pursuit and capture of Geronimo...."

Malone didn't let him continue, his voice taking a sharp edge. "What do you want, Gatewood? Get to the point!"

"What are your intentions here?"

"Don't see as how that's any of your concern, Lieutenant," Clements shot back.

"Anything that happens in this territory is of concern to the military." Gatewood looked at the man's face, taking note of the skull-shaped scar on his cheek. "You're Skull Clements, the notorious gunman."

"Very good, soldier boy!" Joe replied, sarcastically. "For your next trick, care to guess how much money is in my pocket?"

A scattering of snickers could be heard at the comment. The young lieutenant didn't take kindly to looking small in the eyes of his men. He looked around quickly, but his gaze was met by ten sober faces, all staring straight ahead.

Malone sensed what the young officer must be feeling and it touched something inside him. He knew Gatewood had seen the rifle directed at him, yet there had been no fear in his eyes. Grudgingly, he admired the soldier's nerve. He then decided to help the young officer save face.

"Lieutenant, my name is Kellen Malone and you're already acquainted with my friend. We're on our way to Redhawk, peacefully, if at all possible."

"The general wishes to speak with you, Mr. Malone."

"Okay, Lieutenant. We'll ride along with you. But nobody's taking our guns."

One of the soldiers led the way, as Malone and Clements fell in among them. Gatewood brought up the rear. A couple of Indian scouts noticed the tracks left by Malone's horse. Excitedly, they started chattering at each other in Apache. One of them rode up beside the lieutenant and whispered something in his ear.

When they reached the general's position, Gatewood lifted his hand for the soldiers to stop. He proceeded ahead by himself. Speaking to the general in private for a few minutes, he then ordered his troops to escort the men forward.

"Mr. Malone, I am General Nelson A. Miles," he said, ignoring Clements as if he wasn't there. "What is your business here?"

Kell was beginning to grow irritated, increasingly tired of repeating himself. We're making our way through the territory, on our way to Redhawk."

"I understand you've had some trouble with the Apaches."

"I reckon you could call it that, General. They had every intention of lifting my hair, but I've grown kind of attached to it."

Clements laughed at the remark, but   General Miles cast a look of disdain towards the gunman.

"My scouts found where the Chiricahuas attacked you. They called you a mighty warrior, big medicine. They also tell me you killed Running Hawk. Is that so?"

"Well, we were never formally introduced, but Clements said it was Running Hawk. Gave me quite a tussle, General."

"I would imagine he did, Mr. Malone" In spite of himself, Miles smiled at the remark. "I understand there was a twelve year old boy who served with distinction in the Michigan Cavalry Brigade in the War Between the States. They say the young man was half Cherokee. Would that young soldier happen to be you, sir?"

"Yes, General. I served under General George Armstrong Custer."

"I'm pleased to make your acquaintance, Mr. Malone." Then with an obvious look of displeasure, he added, "And I knew George Custer, also."

"With all due respect, General, he was the finest military officer I ever saw and definitely the most courageous."

"Custer was a fool!" Miles exclaimed. "A brave officer, Custer, but a fool nonetheless."

"I think I'm beginning to understand why Clements doesn't like you, Miles."

The general turned to Clements. "I'm surprised they let a murdering cut-throat like you run loose."

Joe's eyes narrowed with hatred. "Wondering the same about you, Miles. Scalp any squaws lately?" Clements looked at his friend. "Malone, the general here likes to hound innocent women and children. Ain't that right, Miles? Shameful what he did to those Cheyenne in the Dakotas. Chased 'em all winter long. Didn't so much as give 'em time to hunt or rest."

"I was just following orders, Clements!"

"Lot of crimes been painted over with those words."

"I've got business to discuss with Mr. Malone. I suggest you leave or be quiet, Mr. Clements, or I will have you placed under arrest."

"I'd like to see you try, soldier boy. Those stripes mean nothing to me!"

The general ignored Joe's remark. "We captured a white trader who was providing whiskey to the Apaches."

"I can clearly see why that would be a concern the military, General."

"Anyway, we have reason to believe someone else has been getting it to the Apaches."

"And why would they want to do that?" Clements interrupted.

Miles threw Clements a look of contempt, but directed his response to Malone. "It is their intention for the Apache to remain hostile, thereby keeping the military around. The troops then purchase things from the traders, swelling their coffers, so to speak."

"Okay, General. But what's this got to do with me?"

"Please walk with me, Malone." Miles walked his horse away from Clements and the soldiers under the general's command. Only when safely out of earshot of the others did he speak. "We think someone in Redhawk is responsible for supplying whiskey to the Apaches."

Malone's eyes narrowed with suspicion. "So I take it this wasn't a chance meeting today?"

"No, sir. I must admit it wasn't. Even Lieutenant Gatewood had no knowledge of my plans." The general wiped the perspiration from his brow with a handkerchief. "We knew about your release from Yuma Prison. If the truth be known, we arranged it."

"Why me?"

"Your ranch."

"My ranch? What's the ranch got to do with it?"

"Is it correct that you have approximately ten thousand acres, some of which borders with Mexico?"

"That's true."

"We believe it is being used as a place to trade with the renegade Chiricahuas. Bordering as it does on Mexico, it would make an excellent location to go unseen. The Apaches," Miles continued, "could cross back and forth across the border undetected. And the bootleggers could continue peddling their wares in both countries. Washington wants the activity stopped. That is where I come in."

"The whole thing makes sense so far, but you know I just got out of prison, General. What makes you think you think you can trust me?"

"You want me to be honest?"

Malone nodded.

"I don't know that we *can* trust you, Malone, but we had to take a chance! Besides, we have reviewed your case. It is our conclusion that you were framed, perhaps for this very reason."

"Sounds like you've spent some time on this."

"I've done my homework, Mr. Malone. We know your reputation as a gunman. We are also familiar with your service record and found it exemplary. My superiors think you're just the man for the job."

"I think you ought to know that my sympathies lie with the Apaches, General. I'm opposed to sending them back east. You see, my mother was a Cherokee. And I'm sure you've heard of the Trail of Tears. I can't help but think this is the same thing all over again."

"Believe me, Mr. Malone, I clearly understand your feelings on this issue. And with all due respect, I do not care what you think!" Miles stared off towards the horizon. "I have my orders already. I am going to capture the renegade, Geronimo! In addition, I'm going to stop these bootleggers and I am asking for your cooperation. However, I fully plan to accomplish these two missions with or without your help!"

"Fair enough. But what do you want me to do?"

"Nothing, Malone. Just listen to see if you hear anything suspicious, anything at all. Although it may seem insignificant, it may be just the clue for which we were searching."

"How will I contact you?"

"You won't. We'll send a man to locate you in couple weeks. Don't worry about spotting him. He'll find you." The general took a drink from his canteen. "This could prove very dangerous, Mr. Malone. I want you to know the risks. The guilty ones may well have spies in our ranks, so there is no one you should trust."

"Trusting other people is a virtue I never embraced."

"Will you help us?"

"Yeah, I'll do what I can, General."

"You will be adequately paid for your services, I assure you."

Malone removed his hat, wiping his brow on his sleeve. He then returned it to his head. "I want more than you're offering."

The general was taken aback. "It appears I have come to the wrong man."

"You misunderstand me, General. This isn't about money. I want the black mark purged from my name." He smiled at General Miles. "The name probably ain't worth much, mind you, but it means more to me than money. Listen, General. I never robbed a stage in my life. Any information the military turned up would be appreciated. And, sir, I would count it as a great personal favor."

"Then you will have it. You have my word!"

As the two men rode back toward the others, Malone said, "I know a little bit about you as well, General. I know that you were wounded twice at Chancellorsville and were awarded the Medal of Honor."

"Ancient history, Mr. Malone."

"I may not agree with your methods, General, but you have earned a measure of my respect."

"For that I thank you." Miles nodded at Joe Clements. "I don't trust that one, Mr. Malone. What is his purpose in traveling to Redhawk with you?"

"Why don't you just ask him, General? I'm not about to ask his business."

"Unlike some, I don't believe in coincidences. Clements turning up just now, headed for Redhawk, just after your release. It's all just a little too pat for me."

"Aw, Miles. You military types are always seeing shadows, even on days when the sun ain't shining," Malone grinned. "I'll be careful, General. Is there anything else?"

"Yes, sir, there is. Sorry to hear about the death of your wife."

"Thank you, General," Malone said, while shaking Miles' hand. "I'll be on my way now. You'll understand if I don't wish you good luck, but I will wish you good health."

Before they returned to the others, the general snapped off his finest military salute to Malone, a gesture normally reserved for officers. "You men are free to go now," Miles said sternly, showing none of the humanity he'd revealed to Malone.

"That's so nice of you, General," said Joe in a cynical tone. He spurred his horse directly ahead, shoving Lieutenant Gatewood's mount out of the way.

As Malone and Clements rode towards the west, the soldiers became simply black dots on the horizon. Only then did Clements say anything.

"What did Miles want?"

"He wanted me to join up with them."

"Smart man, Malone. Never trust anyone wearing a uniform."

Malone looked over at his friend and pulled up on the reins. "If you don't mind me asking, how did you know so much about what General Miles did to the Cheyenne?"

Joe swallowed kind of hard before he answered. "I used to be married to one."

Chapter Three

In a large green, rolling meadow, just back of Clay Adkins' ranch house, a boy and a woolly, coal-black dog were enjoying a game of fetch the stick. The dog answered to the name of Lobo. It was a wolf's name, given to him by Kellen Malone. The boy was known as Jesse.

For those who lived in the area around Redhawk, this flurry of activity behind the house was known as a common sight. The ranch house, rising two stories and overlooking the entire valley, had seen many such games in the past, when it was happily inhabited by Kellen and Alice Malone. Many an hour had been spent in the backyard, man and dog, the games often going long after nightfall, or until the young wife's patience grew thin.

The ranch had been the only home that Lobo ever knew. He had been little more than a playful puppy when his leg became entangled in some trapper's steel device. Fortunately for the dog, a lone, drifting cowhand happened upon him. The kindly, young man brought the wounded animal back to his ranch, slowly nursing him back to health.

The man, called a half-breed by some, had much in common with the dog, for Lobo's pedigree was questionable also. It was this same cowhand who taught the game to the dog. He became a constant companion to the animal, until the men with badges took the man away.

Lobo continued to live with the man's woman and his son. And then, mysteriously to him, the woman vanished as well. They buried her on a stone-marked hillside, just outside of Redhawk. After the burial of the woman, then there was only the boy, Jesse.

The dog was often puzzled about this strange habit these humans had for burial, for it was the same thing he did with the bones he was given.

Another man shared the house with them soon after they placed the woman in the ground. He pretended to be friendly to the animal when people were watching, but the dog knew the man as being cruel, nothing like the gentle cowhand who freed him from the trap. This other man had also made many attempts to rid himself of Lobo, prevented only by the protests of the boy.

The dog was much older now, as was the boy. In spite of the dog's increasing age, he had lost none of his skill at the game. Lobo still took great pleasure in the catching and retrieval of the sawed-off, mop handle. But most of all, he delighted in the boy's futile attempts to wrench it from his iron jaws.

The harder the boy tried to pull the stick from the dog's teeth, the more determined Lobo became to not relinquish possession. It was a new twist to an old game, something invented by the dog, for his own personal delight and entertainment. When the other player, thoroughly frustrated and ready to quit, ceased to pull on the stick, the dog would drop it at the player's feet, ready to start the game again

"Bet you can't catch this one!" Jesse screamed, putting all his weight behind the throw. He threw the stick as far as he possibly could.

Lobo, anticipating the release, was already racing to the place where the stick should land. He leaped high into the air, gracefully catching it between his teeth. It was a feat sharpened with years of practice, one Lobo repeated many times. Unbeknownst to either of the participants, this game had a spectator . . .

Montana Hodges.

Hodges was a man of medium build, with sandy hair that fell to his eyebrows when not under the confines of a hat. He walked with an easy gait, legs bowed slightly.

Although he looked younger than his thirty-three years, those acquainted with Montana thought the last couple of years had not been kind to his features. It was probably due to the imprisonment of his friend, they thought.

Montana's battered chaps slapped against his legs as he walked, a sound that mingled with the jingle of his spurs. His jeans were clean, but showing the wear of many miles in the saddle. A smile came to the young man's face easily, easy as the sun finds the eastern sky at morning. A well-worn revolver rested on his hip. However, on the gentle, soft-spoken cowboy, the six-gun seemed as though it didn't fit the picture.

"Nice catch!" Montana said.

Slightly embarrassed, Jesse turned suddenly, glad to see his friend. "Yeah, Mr. Hodges. Lobo ain't lost his touch."

"How many times do I have to tell you, Jesse? The name's Montana."

"Okay, Mr. Hodges. Or Montana, I mean."

"Now that's more like it," he replied, offering his hand.

As they shook hands, the young cowhand feigned a wince, as if he was in pain. "Getting quite a grip on you, Jesse."

"You really think so, Montana?" the boy asked, swelling with pride. "You said you were going away on business, Montana. When did you get back to Redhawk?"

"I haven't actually gotten back, yet. I stopped off to see you first."

"You mean you came to see me, before anyone else?"

"Yes, sir, I did."

"Nobody ever did anything like that for me before."

Every young boy needs heroes and Jesse Malone was no different. In size and stature, he was quickly approaching manhood, but in his heart and mind, Jesse was still very much the child.

In Montana Hodges, Jesse saw a shining knight of old, riding off to do battle with the cruel, fire-breathing dragon in the stories he'd been told at bedtime. He also saw Montana as the friend and father he never knew.

"Think nothing of it, Jesse."

Lobo wandered over to them, dropping the stick at Jesse's feet, puzzled by the abrupt ending to their game.

"Most folks think I'm too old to be playing kid's games with a dog."

"Not me," Montana said. "Let the fools rage on. A man never grows too old to be kindly to a beast."

Montana took note of the boy's size and resemblance to Kell. "You've really grown since the last time I saw you. Starting to fill out in the chest and shoulders too. You'll probably be bigger than your pa someday, Jesse. It would make him proud, to see how you've turned out, I mean."

Indifferent, Jesse ignored the cowhand's observations about his father.

Hodges leaned over and picked up the stick, before tossing it as far as he could. Lobo barked happily, racing to retrieve it.

"School will be starting in a little bit. Don't you think you ought to be heading that way, before you get your pants dusted?"

"I don't think I'm going to school today," he said, watching the dog run. "I'm almost a man now. Too old to be wasting my time in school."

"Now there's something else a man is never too old to do," Hodges scolded. "You can't ever get too much learning. A man who quits learning might as well die.

"A lot of old folks get the idea that education is just for the young. They're wrong . . . dead wrong! They sit around in a chair, rocking the remainder of their lives away, thinking only of themselves. Then they get bitter and hard, their curiosity about life gone, their desire to learn gone, with no interests to occupy their mind.

"Listen to me, Boy! That's no way to live and a sure way to die. All you have left is plenty of time to discover you added a new wrinkle."

Jesse hung his head in shame and several minutes passed before either of them said another word.

Montana finally broke the silence. "I heard some news the other day. It's something you need to hear."

"What is it?"

"It's about your pa, Jesse. He's going to be released from Yuma. Kell's probably already on his way here."

"So? What's it to me?"

Hodges looked bewildered. "I thought you'd want to know, Jesse. I thought maybe you'd care."

"I don't give a . . ."

"Jesse!" Montana yelled, not giving the boy a chance to finish the sentence. "Watch your language, son! What would your sainted mother think?"

"It don't matter...she's dead anyway. My father saw to that." Jesse paused before throwing the stick to the dog again. "My father is an outlaw and a killer. I wish he was dead!"

"Come on now, Jesse. You don't mean that."

"Yes, I do, Montana. No good as the man was, Ma never stopped defending him to me. Maybe she was just trying to convince herself. Anyway, the shame finally killed her." Jesse looked Hodges in the eye. "Montana, I wish you were my pa. At least you've never lied to me or done anything to hurt my ma. I've always been able to trust you."

Hodges watched the dog catch the stick again, fighting down the lump which came to his throat. "Don't be too hard on him, Jesse. After all, Kell is still your pa."

"No, he ain't! Don't ever call him that! The boy squatted on his haunches, trying to get Lobo to drop the stick. "I know he's your friend, Montana, but he'll never be my pa. He never will!

"Mr. Adkins is my only family now, him and Miss Rachel. They've been good to me, the both of them. Don't know how I could ever repay them." Jesse looked at his friend. "And Miss Rachel...don't she remind you a lot of Ma?"

"Can't argue with you there. She surely does favor Alice."

Montana became quiet and distant for a moment, as though he were turning over a thought in his head. "Come on, boy," Montana said, slipping his arm around Jesse's shoulders. "Take a little walk with me."

The dog trailed along behind them as they walked.

"I've known Kellen Malone for a lot of years, Jesse. He's sided me through a couple of bad scrapes and saved my life more than once. I don't know what would have happened if he wasn't there, but those things aren't what earned my respect for the man."

"Then what does, Montana?"

"Your pa is straight, Son. He's straighter than any man I've ever known. The tracks he leaves on this earth are honest, decent ones. They are tracks a boy would do well to follow.

"Now I don't care what the law said. I don't care what the witnesses said. And most of all, I don't care what Clay Adkins said. Kell is innocent! The man never stole anything in his life. And, Jesse, he loves you. Don't you ever forget that."

Jesse's friend stopped walking when he came to his horse. He loosed the reins from the hitching rail, ducked under, and forked his saddle. "I've got to be going now, Jesse. You'd better be getting yourself to school." Montana smiled at the boy and then tipped his hat. "Promise you'll think about what I've said...will you?"

Jesse didn't reply, but watched with moistened eyes as his friend rode off into the distance.

***

Many consider the desert to be a place shrouded in death, but there is much life to be found amongst the shifting, wind-swept sands. During the rainy season, beautiful flowers spring up in a matter of days, dying quickly as they came.

The vegetation that grows there has long roots, ones that burrow deep, searching for that precious, life-giving moisture. Many creatures also claim the desert as their home, animals wild and untamed as their surroundings.

Wild, untamed, rooted deep in the desert—the words could all be used to describe Kellen Malone. And the man never felt more at peace than when he was in the desert.

As the two horsemen traveled together, Joe Clements had wisely learned to trust Malone's instincts. Kell had developed a certain sense about when they were riding into danger. And those keen instincts became more finely honed with each passing day.

Increasingly, Joe was glad to have him along. Several times, Kell had led them out of sight just before being spotted by the Chiricahuas. And if they were forced to fight, Joe knew that Malone could instantly be transformed from prey to predator.

"What was prison like, Malone?"

Kell thought for a moment before speaking. "As prisons go, I don't guess Yuma was so bad. Worst thing about prison is being caged. Freedom is not something you can see or touch, but it's probably the most precious thing a man owns. Darned shame we so often take it for granted.

"You know, it's kind of funny, Joe. After all this time I walked on this earth, I can't recall thinking about freedom one single time. But for the past seven years, I couldn't think of anything else." Malone stared out over the horizon, looking for signs they were being followed. Only when he was sure they were safe did he speak again. "Looks like we've lost them, for a little while anyway."

"Ain't none of my business, Malone, but how did you end up in Yuma?"

"Stage got robbed in Redhawk. The bandits were all wearing masks, Joe, but my name was used by one of them. After they rode away, someone found my grandfather's watch at their feet," Malone added with a grin. "All pretty convenient, I thought. From there, the rest was easy. In the space of three hours, I was arrested, tried, convicted, and sentenced."

"Did you do it?"

"No, I didn't. But I aim to find out who did! Worst thing about it was the toll it took on Alice. It killed her, Joe." Malone hung his head. "Don't even know what happened to my son. That's why I'm headed for Redhawk."

"We'd better be going, Kell. I'd like to stay ahead of them," Joe grinned. He ran his fingers through his hair. "Look awful hanging on an Apache's belt...don't you think?"

Malone laughed out loud. "Couldn't look any worse than it does now."

Joe was busy rolling a smoke. He took a couple of deep pulls, then smiled from the side of his mouth. "You redskins always stick together."

"I hope Miles don't catch him, Joe."

"Catch who?"

"Geronimo."

"I don't understand you, Malone. Those Chiricahuas nearly lifted your hair a couple of days ago and now you're hoping they get away from the cavalry. You mind explaining that to me?"

"Freedom is the only thing his people have ever known, probably for thousands of years. Now the military wants to take them away from their land and homes, stick them on railcars headed for Florida. Wild things can't live in captivity, Joe. Look what they did to my people, the Cherokee. Nearly wiped them out."

"I know you're right, Malone. Don't guess I've really ever thought on it much. Shame they can't learn to live together and be more tolerant of each other."

"The white man understands nothing of the ways or traditions of the Apache. Men always fear the unknown. What they don't understand, they often seek to destroy." Malone pulled his horse to a stop. He leaned back in the saddle, taking a swallow from his canteen. "For all their high-minded, noble talk, the whites are no better than the Apache. They came to America as a bunch of uninvited guests. Now they've stolen the land away from its rightful owners."

"Kind of makes you wonder who the savages really are," Clements added.

Malone checked the sky and then took one more glance at their back trail. "Well, let's get going, Joe. Time's a wasting."

***

Across the street from the saloon, the wind troubled a broken shutter and the occasional gusts made it clatter against the wall outside an upstairs lawyer's office.

From the outside, the casual observer would see an office of modest simplicity, much the same as any struggling Western attorney would choose to hang his shingle. Significant only by its insignificance, little had been done to improve its features. The humble appearance was clearly by design, a deliberate attempt to draw attention away from the activities which took place within its walls.

Once inside the door, a visitor could see a spacious room, one which bore no resemblance to its meager exterior. The beautiful office was enhanced with fine furniture and expensive works of art. A hand-crafted, oaken desk was the centerpiece of the room.

One of the walls was lined with bookshelves, most of them law books, but also containing leather bound copies of the works of Shakespeare, Tennyson, and others. These were hardly the trappings of a typical honest, Western attorney . . .

Lawyer Carlton Stadler was none of these.

Stadler was a man of threadbare morals and questionable virtue. The law that he practiced was as shady as the details of his past. No one had any clue as to Carlton's birthplace. And even had it been considered good manners, few men would have worked up the courage to question him about it.

Some said Stadler was a gunfighter, a man come west to escape his past. This rumor was given some substance because of the man's ever-present revolver. He merely dismissed it as a necessity of his vocation, always dealing with criminals and the lawless. Then there were the trips. The lawyer would disappear for days at a time, always making a large bank deposit upon his return to town.

Stadler had come to Redhawk about seven years ago. He stepped from the stage carrying a couple of law books and a worn carpet bag. Most noticeable of all, a six-gun hung on his hip, one that showed more than its share of use.

The lawyer's first case had been the defense of Kellen Malone. The trial was held at the saloon and presided over by a traveling court judge. As did most trials, the legal proceedings drew a huge crowd from all over the territory.

Lawyers of the period had been known to develop a large and loyal following, often praised for their oratory as much as their trial skills.

Most presented their closing arguments fervently, in much the same way as a minister appeals to his congregation. But those expecting grand words in Malone's behalf went away greatly disappointed. Stadler presented a weak, uninspired defense, one that impressed none of the onlookers.

The following day, a shackled Kellen Malone was put on a prison wagon, bound for Yuma Territorial Prison...

And Carlton Stadler placed his next large deposit.

The wind continued to worry the broken shutter outside his office. Normally a nuisance, it now went unnoticed.

Carlton Stadler, lost in study and carefully poring over a territorial map, sank deeply into his well-upholstered desk chair. A glass of brandy rested beside him. The lawyer paid special attention to the area bordering the town of Redhawk. Then a knock on the door interrupted his concentration.

"Come on in," Stadler shouted, the gun springing to his hand.

The door burst open quickly, revealing the face and massive body of Clay Adkins. Staring down the gaping bore of the lawyer's six-gun, Clay turned as pale as a corpse.

"You're a cautious man, Stadler."

"Caution must always be a watchword of the living," Carlton observed before holstering his gun.

Clay nodded, sensing a great profundity in the man's simple statement.

"And to what do I owe this pleasure, Mr. Adkins?" A tinge of sarcasm rang in the lawyer's voice. "I thought you'd be busy making wedding preparations with the lovely, Miss Payton. I hope there has been no change in your plans. Any man would be envious of a chance to slip a halter on that filly."

Adkins cared little for the lawyer's sly comments about his fiancée, his statements routinely becoming more commonplace. For now, he deliberately chose to ignore them.

"We have to do something, Carl," Clay blustered, his voice trembling slightly. "Malone is to be released from prison today."

"Is that so?" Stadler replied, tossing down the last of his brandy. He rose from the chair and poured himself another. "Care for a shot, Clay? You sure look like you could use one."

"Yes, thank you," he said, accepting the drink. Clay tasted the brandy and spoke again. "If Malone comes back here, it will spoil everything, your plans and mine. Everything will be spoiled by a worthless, two-bit saddle tramp."

"But I thought you said Malone would be killed trying to escape. The guard's name was Dotson, wasn't it? If I accurately recall all the details, he was handsomely paid to eliminate the problem."

"And he would have, had it not been for the superintendent, Frank Ingalls. Dotson and I had the whole thing set up. When Malone escaped, which I felt sure he would, Dotson would make sure he never got back alive. Ingalls wouldn't stand for anything like that."

Clay took another drink of the brandy. He could feel his courage and clarity of thought return as the liquor warmed his insides. "The superintendent didn't even increase the half-breed's sentence for his failed escape. All he got out of it was a beating and a couple of weeks in the dark cell." Adkins cursed under his breath.

"Sure makes you wonder what kind of a prison they're running out there!" Adkins fumed. "I hear Yuma now gives each prisoner an allotment of a pound and a half of beef per day. Guards eat the same thing the prisoners do. Rehabilitation of the prisoners, they call it. Bah!" Adkins muttered bitterly. "Sounds more like a ladies' quilting bee."

"Get a grip on yourself, Clay. So far, nearly everything has gone just the way you planned it."

Adkins threw a suspicious glare in the lawyer's direction. "And what makes you think you are so intimately acquainted with my plans?"

Stadler leaned back in his chair, folding his arms smugly. "The papers will be finalized in a matter of days, weeks at the most. Arizona's circuit court will appoint you Jesse's legal guardian. The beautiful Miss Payton will soon be your wife. Then, Malone's ranch will be yours, ten thousand acres with some of the finest graze in the territory. How am I doing so far?"

"You missed one thing. All these things are dependent on Kellen Malone being out of the picture."

"It's several days ride from Yuma Prison to Redhawk. A lot of things can happen to a man in that length of time, Clay. A horse could throw him. He might die of thirst. Maybe the Apaches will get to him. Geronimo and Running Hawk both claim all that area as their own, you know." Stadler's lips parted in a self-satisfied smile.

The look did not go without notice. "What is it, Carl? You look like the cat that just ate the canary."

Carlton leaned forward in his chair, hands folded. "Malone will never make it back to Redhawk alive," he grinned. "And, Carl, dead men are never a problem."

"What are you talking about?"

"Indians. The Apaches," Stadler explained. "Running Hawk was all too happy to kill a white man. Better yet to get paid for it. By nightfall, Mr. Kellen Malone will be nothing more than a bad memory and a bloody scalp hanging from an Apache's belt." Stadler laughed viciously, a humorless amusement that made Adkins question the lawyer's sanity. "Those savages will do almost anything for a new rifle and a little whiskey."

"How did you manage to set that deal up, Carl? Come to think of it...never mind. I'm not sure I want to know." Adkins pulled a cigar from his inner breast pocket. He bit off the end, then spat it out. Stadler offered him a light. "Thanks, Carl."

"You're much too squeamish, Clay. I don't like weakness in a man. It's a poor character trait, something that can be exploited. It makes a person careless, jumpy, even dead. Maybe you should just forget this whole thing and turn it over to someone with the stomach for it." The lawyer's blue-gray eyes twinkled crazily. "And I'd be more than happy to take that Payton woman off your hands."

Another one of Stadler's vile references to Rachel—the thought made Clay's soul boil. He fought the temptation to go for his gun, probably just the thing Carlton wanted.

Clay took a couple of puffs, deeply, thoughtfully. "Ever since you came to this town, I've relied on your help. And even you must admit, Carlton, it has been a profitable venture for both of us." Adkins chose his words carefully, having no desire to incur the wrath of the gunslinger turned lawyer.

"You go ahead and take care of the final details involving the ranch," Clay said. "Just don't get any foolish ideas about who's in charge! I'm the one who keeps up the fancy lifestyle that you seem to love so much. Without me, you'd have to go back to selling out your gun to the highest bidder. Neither of us wants that. But if you become a liability to me, then...."

"That had all the making of a threat, Clay. I don't like threats and you're in no position to be giving them. Don't forget one thing...you need me, Clay.

"I'm the one who saw that Malone got a less than adequate defense. I know all about the gold watch, where it came from, and how it was planted at the stage robbery. I know other things, too. I have knowledge of things you want kept secret." Stadler sank back in his chair, obviously pleased with himself. "I know too much, Adkins."

The lawyer took another sip of his brandy. "The court will appoint you to be Jesse Malone's legal guardian in a matter of days or weeks. With Kellen Malone dead, there will be no one left to muddy the waters. All of his possessions will go to his only living heir, Malone's son. That will put you in control of all of it...the woman, the ranch, and everything. And if some misfortune should befall the boy—as I'm sure it will—all of it reverts to you. Am I correct?"

Clay Adkins swallowed hard, realizing for the first time he had underestimated Carlton Stadler. The man was smart, certainly too smart for his own good. The man is right, Adkins thought, I do need him...at least for now.

A cloud of imposing death hung heavy in the room. Both of the men recognized their immediate need for each other, but when that need no longer existed...

"Don't get any funny ideas," Stadler muttered coldly, as if reading the other man's thoughts. "I could kill you, Adkins, real easy. Never even work up a good sweat."

Clay rose from his chair and started for the door. "I know I am clearly no match for you with a gun, yet I have men in my employment who are. They are completely loyal to me. Some of them would think nothing of shooting a man in the back. Is my meaning clear?" Adkins paused in the doorway. "I'm top dog around here, Carl. You'd do well to remember it!" Clay stormed out the door, slamming it behind him.

Moments after Adkins left Stadler's office, another knock sounded gently on the door. "Come on in," the lawyer hollered. "I've been expecting you."

The stranger looked both ways, making sure that no one was watching before he entered the office. An easy smile came to the man's face and humor danced in his eyes. "I had to wait until Adkins left. It wouldn't be good for us to be seen together."

This latest visitor plunked himself down on one of Stadler's finest easy chairs. Feeling the lawyer's cold stare upon him, he removed his spurs. "The least you could do is offer me a drink. You gave him one."

Carlton looked disgusted as he poured the man a drink. "I'm not paying you just to drink my liquor and ruin my furniture with your spurs."

"I've done everything you asked, Mr. Stadler. But I have to admit that it kind of leaves me with a bad taste in my mouth."

The lawyer handed him a snifter of brandy and an envelope filled with money. "Maybe these will help to wash away the taste."

He stuck the money in his pocket and took a sip from his drink. "Seems like an awful big glass for this small amount," he replied, draining it in one swallow.

Stadler didn't appreciate the man's home-spun humor, but he did appreciate the work he had covertly done for him. Carlton poured the man another. "This, my friend, is not like the beer you swill at the Lady Luck.

"Brandy is meant to be savored slowly, like a beautiful woman." He raised the glass, swirling the liquid around in the light. "First, you observe the way it gently moves. Next you enjoy the pleasures of its sweet bouquet. Last of all, you sip it slowly, leisurely, enjoying every sensation." The lawyer stared blankly into space, conjuring up images of the woman at the diner. "Well, what did you find out?" he asked, returning to himself.

The visitor eyed him strangely before speaking. "You were right about one thing, Mr. Stadler. Adkins did decide to hire himself some help. He sent a couple of telegrams out this morning. One of them went to a man named Dotson, but I don't know who that is. I'm guessing you do though."

"Dotson used to be a guard at the prison. What about the other telegraph?"

"He also sent a telegram to Skull Clements, the gunman."

"Skull Clements. Now that's interesting!" The lawyer was familiar with the man's name and reputation.

"Yeah," the stranger replied, tossing down his drink. "You've got to give the man credit. He only hires the best."

Carlton Stadler pondered over this latest information. He knew Clements was a meticulous, stone-faced killer, a gunman of the old school. He liked to kill men facing him. "Joe Clements doesn't work cheap," the lawyer said, thinking out loud. "I knew Clay wanted Malone out of the way, but not that bad."

"Clements has done some work for Adkins in the past. It ain't all that surprising that he would contact him again."

The lawyer nodded, still in thought.

"One other thing you might want to consider, Mr. Stadler."

"And what would that be?"

"Maybe Skull is coming for more than just Malone. Not many men could beat him to the draw. Maybe you couldn't either. Adkins could still have plans on cutting you out of the herd too."

"I like the way you think. You're smart, much too smart to be a common cowhand," Stadler said, immediately sensing the logic in the young man's thinking. "Like I said before, I want to know where he goes, what he does, and who he talks to. You'd better go now. And use the back door this time! I can't risk you being seen. Your value to me rests in your ability to move freely and undetected."

"Don't worry about me, Mr. Stadler. I know which side my bread is buttered on." He leaned over in his chair and strapped on his spurs. The young man then came to his feet, pulling the drapery to one side before peering out the window. "I'll see you later," he said, tipping his hat.

The door closed behind him.

"Adkins—top dog! We'll just see about that," Carlton muttered, then laughing to himself crazily. "The fool! Top dog is the one left holding the bone."

Chapter Four

Rachel Payton was just completing the last of her morning's daily cleaning. Unlike some women, Rachel had always relished the rigors of house cleaning and took great pleasure in a job well done.

Always mindful of her appearance, Rachel fussed with her hair while stopping to admire her handiwork. It was a lovely home, she thought. Soon it would truly be hers and she would share its many comforts with her fiancé, Clay Adkins.

Many of the locals thought Rachel resembled the late Mrs. Kellen Malone. Yet the woman was beautiful in her own right and lovely in face and form, with her fine auburn hair falling about shoulder length.

There was an inner beauty to the woman, a quality which fought its way to the surface, refusing to be hidden underneath. And beautiful she was, although Rachel never thought of herself as being so. Strangers passing her on the street usually found themselves taking a second look. Rachel found it flattering, yet embarrassing at the same time.

Clay had been more than kind to her in these past few months, insisting that she stay in his ranch house. He had then chosen to rent a room in Redhawk, to avoid any appearance of impropriety. It was certainly a noble thing he did, almost chivalrous.

It reminded Rachel of the fairy tales her father told her as a child. She had not expected such hospitality when she arrived here—not from a stranger—not in this part of the west.

After selling everything they owned in Virginia, Rachel moved to the Arizona territory with her father. "The west," he declared, "is a place where a man can become as big as the land itself and go as far as his dreams will take him."

The way her father talked about the west made it seem magical and romantic to a young woman. His descriptions of this far away land made Rachel long to see it also.

No one could have predicted the Apaches' attack on the stage or the stray arrow that took her father's life.

Those who knew such things claimed that Geronimo and Running Hawk were nowhere in the territory at the time of the attack. The "experts" were wrong. Whooping and hollering, the Chiricahuas came down out of the hills, sweeping down upon the stage. As was their custom, it was the last place anyone would ever suspect an attack.

The shotgun guard and several of the passengers got off shots at the Apache raiding party. Rachel had even downed one of the braves with a well-placed shot from her father's Henry rifle. A couple of the passengers were wounded, none seriously. The attack finally broke when the strong team of stage horses began to outdistance the smaller Indian ponies.

Almost as a final act of defiance, Running Hawk randomly let fly another arrow. As fate would have it, the arrow entered the stagecoach's window, killing Rachel's father. The passengers buried him at the next station, in a shallow grave next to the stage line.

Rachel Payton, stricken with grief, continued on her way to Redhawk.

A woman traveling alone was not likely to receive a hearty welcome in a place like Redhawk. Vocations were clearly limited for a woman. The jobs to be had were not readily desired by someone of high moral fiber. It wasn't too long before Rachel became the target of suspicious stares and cruel gossip. During the roughest times, she kept mostly to herself. Clay Adkins was the first man who truly befriended her.

As time passed, the harsh looks grew softer and the whispered remarks grew less venomous. Hatred and fear are burdens which grow heavier with the miles. The local women, no longer feeling threatened by her presence, began casting those weights aside. Increasingly, the lightened loads made the journey less difficult for everyone.

Rachel Payton had finally come home.

In the time to follow, Clay continued to call on her, the visits soon increasing in frequency and duration. During one of these visits, Adkins asked for Rachel's hand in marriage. Grateful for all the kindnesses he directed her way, the woman happily accepted his proposal.

Rachel walked to the mirror, holding the wedding gown in front of herself to imagine how it would look. It was a beautiful dress. Until recently, she rarely thought of Mama, but her mother's dress brought all the old memories flooding back. She had died when Rachel was a child and it bothered her sometimes that she couldn't clearly remember her mother's face.

Papa used to smile when she made the statement. "Stand in front of the mirror," he liked to say. "Put on your prettiest smile and you'll be looking at a picture of your mother."

The memory of Papa's words never failed to brighten her day.

A wedding is a special time, a nearly sacred ritual to be shared between mother and daughter. Rachel wished her mother could have lived for this day. Her mind was filled with all the hope, joy, and anticipation of a woman about to be wed. There were plans to be made, last minute details requiring her attention. Rachel dearly wanted to share these things with somebody. She had no one.

Suddenly the question came to her. Who would walk her down the aisle, offering her hand to the man she would share her life with? Who?

A tear came to her eye as she remembered the fine man who had been her father. He was a good man, tough as nails, with a gentle side seen only by Rachel and her mother. Rachel had always been wise enough to place great value in his opinion.

Her father knew men and understood their ways.

As certain as she was about her choice, still, something inside her doubted. There was an uncertainty about Clay. Perhaps it was a feeling or instinct, something she couldn't explain. Rachel told herself these feelings were normal for this time in a woman's life. At the same time, her mind refused to believe it. She wished her father were with her now, to share in her joy...but mostly, to affirm her decision.

Rachel looked out the window, longingly gazing towards the horizon, her mind lost on a memory. It was then she saw the two riders off in the distance.

***

Malone and Clements urged their horses along the gently curving road towards the ranch. As Kell got closer to his home place, his mind was filled with images of Alice and Jesse, along with the memories of happier times.

Malone remembered all the hard work he put into building the house and the doubts that showed in her eyes along the way. Alice carried tools while he worked on the structure. He smiled as he recalled the time he busted his thumb with a hammer. Alice tried to hold her laughter, but the humor finally got the better of her.

When the ranch house was finished, it was a warm, comfortable place, one in which they could both be proud. It was then that Alice told him about the baby she was carrying. The two of them sat on the front steps, holding one another, laughing like children.

As Kell remembered the happy times they once enjoyed, he cursed softly.

"What's that you say?"

"Nothing, Joe. Nothing at all."

Approaching the ranch house, Kell was surprised to see the building in such fine condition. He found it strange. So far as he knew, no one should have been living there. A quick look around told him otherwise.

Malone wasn't the only one to notice. "That surely don't look like an empty house," Joe observed.

"Beats me," Malone replied, bewildered.

"Must be someone living there," Joe said. "House sits empty, it gets run down and falls apart quick. Never have understood why. It just seems to work that way."

The shutters were all hanging level, something they hadn't done when Malone went to prison. The fences were in good repair, all freshly whitewashed. A woman's touch could be seen around the ranch also. Alice had always loved flowers and those she planted were well-cared for and blooming. Kell sniffed at the air. He could smell baked apples and cinnamon. The scent took him back to another time.

Grateful as Malone was for the work done around the place, he still resented someone moving in without his permission. It was his house, a place built with his own hands. Kell had many precious memories there and he wouldn't allow some intruder to steal that which rightfully belonged to him.

Drawing closer, a large, black dog came charging towards them. The animal was barking fiercely. Kell smiled, recognizing the dog immediately. It was Lobo.

Joe's horse, spooked by the dog's sudden charge, began to buck wildly, rearing high into the air, nearly loosing Clements from the saddle. Joe pulled hard at the reins, finally bringing the animal under control. He fouled the air with profanity and started to pull his gun.

"How're you doing, boy," Kell said, glad to see his pet. "It's been a long time."

Bewildered, Clements eased his gun back into the holster. "You know this mutt?"

"Yea, Lobo and I are old friends."

"I dang near shot him."

"Real bad idea, Joe. You remember what happened to Running Hawk back there. And I wasn't even mad at him."

Clements smiled. "I'll keep that in mind."

At the sound of a familiar voice, Lobo's barking stopped and his tail began wagging. With a powerful leap, the dog thrust himself into Kell's lap. It was a habit Lobo acquired many years ago, whenever his master returned to the ranch on horseback. The dog had not forgotten.

The dog's unexpected action frightened Kell's horse. With a gentle pat on the neck, some kind words, and a firm grip on the reins, Malone calmed his mount. Grudgingly, the horse accepted the dog's uncommon behavior and the added burden on his back.

Joe eyed Malone strangely, a look of curiosity in his eyes. "Mite big for a lap dog," he said, no longer able to contain himself.

Kell just grinned and continued riding towards the house. Lobo sat across his lap, licking at his face.

"Had a woman like that once," muttered Joe.

When Rachel Payton saw the two strangers from the window, she assumed they were a pair of drifting cowhands, grub liners looking for a warm meal and some pleasant conversation. She had seen many of them in her short time here. Lonely men they were, tired of long trail drives and their own cooking. Some of them were in search of odd jobs, if there were any to be had. Their arrival was always welcomed. Visitors carried information, news from other towns and places, something she now missed.

As Rachel made her way to the front door, she was puzzled by the dog's sudden silence. A good watchdog, Lobo always made a racket when strangers came. Silence was a characteristic usually reserved for Rachel's friends or people known by the dog. Yet she had not recognized the horses. Casting a quick glance above the fireplace, Rachel saw the gun was still hanging there. It was a good thing to know.

Joe waited next to the barn, still astride his horse. He made no effort to come any closer, even at Malone's invitation.

"Come on in, Joe."

"Thanks, but I think I'll wait here. Maybe have me a smoke." There was sort of hesitancy in his manner, like someone fearful of intruding. "You be careful, Malone. Hard to tell who's in there."

"Already thought of that," Malone said. "Never did know an outlaw to grow flowers or a thief taking time to tidy up."

"Probably right about that. Always a first time, though. Never hurts to be too careful." His horse dropped its neck to crop grass. Joe smiled politely and fumbled for his tobacco sack.

As he neared the house, Kell paused a moment to take it all in. Returning home was always special to him, but never more so than at this moment. Prison takes a lot out of a man, maybe more than he can afford to lose. Seven long years of his life were gone. He once thought nothing would make him feel this good again. Why must a man lose something to appreciate what he has?

Kell breathed deeply, taking in the fresh air. Then he started up the steps. Joe was right. Somebody had to be inside. He loosed the gun in its holster, just to be ready.

"Jesse, Frank, and the Younger brothers could all be inside," he mumbled, "and all their relatives. The place would still be empty without Alice."

He wondered if the ranch house would ever be anything more than the empty shell it was now. Alice had been the one who transformed the place into a home.

Rachel pushed back the lace curtain on the window and peered outside. The man dismounted, leaving his reins hanging. Rachel carefully studied the man as he walked towards the ranch house. From the man's dress and appearance, she took him for a cowhand. His clothes were stained with sweat and trail dust, boots run down, his hat battered and weary.

The stranger was tall, lean of face and form, and rugged. The shirt he wore did nothing to hide his heavily muscled shoulders, the fabric of his shirt stretched taut. Rachel knew this man had been no stranger to hard work.

Something in his manner told her this stranger could name every detail around him. He looked straight ahead, eyes darting, seeing nothing, yet seeing everything. The man walked proudly, like a person who knew where he was going in life. Every step taken was sure and confident. It was a quality Rachel remembered in her father.

Malone started to walk on into the house as he had always done. Then catching himself, he raised a clenched fist towards the door. Kell thought a man shouldn't have to knock before entering his own home. Just then, the door swung open. The face in the doorway left Kell startled, completely taken aback.

"May I help you?" asked the woman at the door.

"Alice...?" Kell asked tentatively, amazed at the striking resemblance between this woman and his wife, his late wife.

"No," she replied. "My name is Payton. Rachel Payton."

"I'm sorry, Ma'am. It's just—it's just you looked kind of familiar. You remind me of someone I used to know. For a minute there, I thought you were my...my...a friend."

Kell wasn't sure why he'd said nothing about this woman resembling his dead wife. His reasoning was something he couldn't fully put into words. Malone had no desire to reveal too much of himself, not to this intruder. First, he must learn Miss Payton's reason for being there.

"I wish I was."

Hers was a strange response. Although Malone wasn't sure it was meant that way, it sounded almost forward of her. He thought he detected a hint of blush to her cheeks. After a couple seconds of further study, he was sure of it.

"We don't get many visitors around here," she muttered, the embarrassment still showing in her face.

"No, I don't suppose you do."

"Forgive me for my manners. You look like you've been riding for a long time. Tell your friend to come inside and I'll make you both something to eat." Rachel smoothed down her hair, suddenly worried about her appearance. "I've also got some coffee and a hot apple pie cooling in the window."

Kell, startled by the woman's appearance, had almost forgotten the smell. "You make it sound mighty tempting, ma'am. Thanks anyhow. We can't stay. I'm looking for my son."

Rachel was curious. "That doesn't sound like something a man should misplace?" she replied, fishing for an explanation.

Kell smiled, knowingly. He had tossed out a line or two of his own on occasion. Desperate for information, Kell needed to do a little fishing of his own right now. "Well, I've been gone for quite some time," he said, still revealing nothing.

Doubt showed in her eyes, uncertainty as to whether the question had been dodged intentionally. She studied his face.

Malone tried to look innocent.

"What made you think he'd be here?"

"He used to live in this house with his parents."

She nodded her head. "I'm sure you are mistaken, sir. The man who built this house went to prison. Yuma, I think. The place was purchased from his widow, Alice Malone, God rest her soul."

"Purchased you say?"

"That's right. My fiancé bought it a couple of years ago. Your son couldn't have lived here."

"So you're living in your fiancé's house? I see."

Kell eyed her strangely, knowing this was no proper arrangement for a lady. Men and women didn't share houses without the benefit of clergy. Even though he'd been behind bars for seven years, he was sure society's moral acceptance hadn't changed that much. Still, he considered it none of his business.

"I'm afraid you don't see!" Rachel fumed, angered by what she saw as the stranger's assumption about her decency. "My fiancé allows me to live here. That's all! He's staying in the hotel at Redhawk. I assure you there is no impropriety in my behavior."

"I didn't say there was, ma'am."

"Yes, but don't tell me you didn't think it." Rachel said, glaring at the stranger. "My fiancé is an honorable man." Her chin lifted proudly. "Mr. Adkins wouldn't permit my reputation to be questioned."

"Who did you say?"

"Mr. Clay Adkins." Her eyes lit up. "Do you know him?"

At the first mention of the name, Malone felt the anger and hatred building up inside him. His fists clenched longingly.

"Yeah, I know him. I've heard Adkins called a lot of things, some I can't repeat in front of a lady. Don't ever recall one of the names being honorable."

Her gaze turned cold. "At least he's a gentleman, which is more than I can say for you. And besides, what do you know of him?"

"Just say I know him."

"No matter," she replied. "Your welcome is done here. I would suggest you not be on this ranch when he arrives."

"You would, would you?"

Rachel nodded, her jaw set firm. Then she turned to go.

"About the woman who sold you the house . . ." Kell said, scratching his head. His inquiry stopped the woman in the door. "What became of her husband, the man who built the house? And what makes you think he won't be coming back to Redhawk?"

Rachel wondered about the stranger's great interest in local affairs. "He won't be back. That I'm sure of! Malone was killed a couple of days ago. The Apaches got him, or so they say. It happened right after his release from Yuma Prison."

Malone was confused. Something mysterious was going on here. From the woman's answers, Kell figured she had no idea what Adkins was doing. And knowing the man as he did, Malone knew it could be nothing good.

"Well, if Clay knows the whereabouts of my son, tell him to contact me. I'll be staying in Redhawk."

"Where?"

"I won't be hard to find." Malone turned to leave, then stopped. "By the way, tell Adkins that he has one week to clear off this ranch. And if you insist on marrying him, Miss Payton, the same goes for you."

"Wait a minute!" Rachel sputtered. "First, you come riding up to the ranch, asking all kinds of question, most of which are none your business. You insulted me and my fiancé. Then you have the nerve to accuse us of concealing your son and order us to leave our home." Rachel's face turned beet red. "Now you plan to ride away without so much as an explanation. Is there anything else I can do for you?" she replied, sarcastically.

"Yes, there sure was, ma'am, but I figured a kiss was going to be out of the question."

The remark left her speechless, a condition which lasted but a moment. "You are definitely the most arrogant man I've ever met! Clay will have you horsewhipped for your insolence. Who should I tell him to see?"

"Begging your pardon, ma'am." Kell swept the hat from his head, bowing low before her. "My name is Malone, the *late* Mr. Kellen Malone."

Rachel's face turned a deathly white. "You can't be Malone! He's dead. I saw them bringing the body into town."

"Sorry to disappoint everyone, but it wasn't me."

The woman was at a loss for words.

"When Clay comes to whip me," Kell explained, "make sure he comes with plenty of help. He'll be sure to need it. Besides, dead men are hard to kill."

Malone mounted his horse, urging it alongside the verandah. For a moment, he stared at the woman while saying nothing. It was a measuring glance, intended to learn something of the woman's character and breeding. Much can be learned from the eyes, for in them the soul is stripped bare. There was honesty in her eyes. Depth was there also, like a fine spirited horse. This woman would be someone to ride the river with, and strong enough to face whatever came down the trail to meet them.

Silently, she watched Malone.

"And one more thing," he said, breaking the silence. "Alice hated Clay Adkins...almost as much as I do. She wouldn't sell him a swayback nag, let alone this ranch. Take my advice, Miss Payton. Don't harness yourself to a liar."

"I don't recall asking for your advice!" she flared. "And you're wrong about Mr. Adkins."

"Am I, Rachel?"

Still, she said nothing.

The dog nudged Kell's leg with its nose. "Lobo, you stay put. I'll be back for you later. We'll play then."

Lobo did as he was told, his jaws clenching the tooth-worn, sawed-off mop handle. His eyes took on a look of sadness and disappointment, staring forlornly at his master.

"Okay. Okay," Malone said. "But just this once." He took the stick from the dog's teeth, flinging it as far as he could. The black animal raced after it, barking contentedly. Saying nothing further, Kell swung up into his saddle. Reining the horse around, he galloped off towards Joe.

Joe sat there waiting, his lips turned up in a wry smile. "So I take it you've got some boarders?"

"Just one, Joe...some she-cat named Rachel Payton. Mean as Satan himself. She might even be ornery as you."

"That bad, huh?"

"The woman claims she's engaged to the new owner. Says he's staying in Redhawk, letting her use the house."

"You didn't tell me you sold it."

"I didn't, Joe. Neither did Alice."

"But she says otherwise?" Joe asked, while calmly rolling another smoke.

"That's about the size of it."

Joe shoved the cigarette between his lips, striking a match on his saddle. It flared up inside his cupped hand. "Who bought the house?" he muttered, taking a couple of deep puffs.

"Clay Adkins...the man I plan to kill."

Clements choked on the name, almost swallowing his cigarette. "I can't let you do that, Malone."

Kell's gaze turned cold. "And why not?"

"Cause I didn't ride all this way for nothing. Adkins is the one who hired me, Malone. He's got a job waiting for me in Redhawk."

Malone suddenly remembered that Clay had paid Dotson to kill him. An idea suddenly came to his mind. If Adkins wanted him dead that much, Clements might be his ace in the hole, a back-up in case Dotson failed. "I wouldn't take the job, Joe."

"What makes you say that?"

"Nothing really. I just got a hunch you won't like the work. Besides, I'm not sure you're up to it."

"I'll be the judge of that," Joe snapped back.

Silently, he studied Malone's face the way he would read the eyes of a man about to draw on him. The look revealed nothing. Although he couldn't understand what just happened, Joe felt there was a reason, some hidden undercurrent behind Malone's sudden interest in his job.

"Suit yourself. I just hope you don't get on the wrong side of things, Joe. I wouldn't look with favor on killing you."

"Neither would I, Malone."

The two riders started their horses walking up the trail towards town. Although side by side, there was a distance between them. Malone was first to bridge the gap.

"That isn't all, Joe. There's more. The woman said the Apaches got me a couple of days ago. I'm supposed to be dead."

"I imagine you took the news pretty hard, no one telling you and all." Joe roared with laughter. "Let me see if I got this straight. There's a woman living in a house you ain't sold. The Apaches killed you but you ain't dead. You've sworn to kill a man, but I ain't gonna let you. Guess things could get a whole lot worse."

"Worse? How do you figure it could get any worse?"

Joe spoke from the side of his mouth, talking around the cigarette clenched in his lips. "That woman back there...she could have been ugly like me."

"What makes you think she wasn't?"

"Let me tell you something about myself, Malone. Deaf and dumb...maybe. Mean and cantankerous... definitely. But blind and stupid . . . not on your life!"

"Come on, Joe. Let's get going."

"Right behind you, Malone," he smiled, flicking the cigarette away. Clements studied the attractive woman still standing outside the ranch house. "No, sir. Nothing wrong with my eyesight at all!" Joe slapped the spurs to his mount, soon catching up with his friend.

As Kell rode away, he couldn't resist stealing another look over his shoulder. Rachel was still there. She stood in front of the house, shielding her eyes from the sun. Malone still couldn't believe how much she looked like Alice.

After just receiving the woman's bitter scolding, he found himself strangely angry. He wondered why he should care what Rachel Payton thought. She was no concern of his. And what did it matter to him who she married?

It was not the first dressing-down a woman had given him. Many had been the time Alice found occasion to talk to Kell that way. He wondered why it should bother him. Like Alice, the woman also had a fire to her. His mind puzzled over the questions for a time, finally deciding to give the matter no further consideration. But still...

Joe said nothing as they rode along.

Malone was glad.

***

Rachel was angered by the man's attitude, which she perceived as arrogant and abrasive. "Lobo, I wish you'd bitten him," she muttered, knowing she didn't mean the words. She watched in confused silence as the two strangers became dark specks in the distance. Had the man looked back? Rachel was sure he did. Then she wondered why she should care.

So this was Jesse's father, she thought. Malone was nothing like the man she expected—except for the arrogance. Rachel thought she should be angry for the way he spoke to her and she certainly wanted to be. Yet something about the man made it impossible for Rachel to sustain her rage.

She had heard all the stories about the notorious Kellen Malone, the stage he robbed and the men he killed. In her mind, the man didn't look like a thief. Rachel admitted that she knew little about such things, even with all her father taught her. And what of the killings? Almost all men carried guns in the West.

Rachel realized that she never thought of them as being anything other than a matter of dress. Surely they must use them at times. Did she not shoot one of the Indians from the stagecoach? Maybe it had been the same for him and he'd merely been forced to protect himself. However, with the reputation he carried, she thought it unlikely.

Rachel remembered how the man looked at her, how he said she resembled someone he knew. Why had he said that? She wondered what the stranger must think of her after she sounded so forward. She hoped the man didn't notice the blush it brought to her cheeks. Still, she believed nothing escaped his attention. Strange as it seemed, Rachel knew she had been truthful with the man. She did wish this seemingly arrogant stranger considered her a friend.

Malone's gaze left her feeling strangely excited. Emotions were stirred inside her heart, feelings she couldn't understand or hope to put into words.

There was a quality about Malone which touched something deep within her. Long-dormant chords of feeling were softly stroked by his gentle voice and lonely eyes. Then she remembered Clay, her fiancé. Feelings of guilt swept over her, embarrassment and shame. She believed a woman about to be married shouldn't feel this drawn to a total stranger.

Rachel dismissed these strange emotions as simple loneliness. Her father and mother were dead, and she missed them deeply. Doubts are a normal thing for a woman before her wedding. And what else could they be?

Another matter troubled her. Clay said Malone had been killed by the same Apaches who murdered her father. How could he have possibly known that? And why would he say such a thing when it was so obviously wrong? She considered the matter for a time, then dismissed it. It was probably just bad information. I must think to ask him later, she thought.

Rachel shielded her eyes towards the sun, still watching the two riders. When Malone disappeared into the horizon, she felt empty—lost. The sudden feeling was clearly a mystery to her.

Chapter Five

The day was sunny and bright, not a cloud in the wide, blue Arizona sky. Two weeks had come and gone since the last drop of rain had fallen. However, another kind of storm was about to descend on this quiet community, as a pair of bone-weary travelers drifted into the town of Redhawk.

The shirts the men were wearing were sweat-stained and pungent, bearing no memory of the days when they were fresh, clean, and new. A hot bath and a strong bar of soap ranked high on the newcomers' list of priorities, preceded only by a good, cold beer. Both of these items took second place behind caring for their faithful horses.

The arrival of strangers through this insignificant, Western town was not an uncommon occurrence. It was calmly noted by the local, then ignored...until now.

As the two men urged their horses down the normally tranquil, city street, they found themselves the object of suspicion, their every move met by curious stares. To the casual observer, the strangers might be mistaken for drifting cowhands, ordinary drovers in search of strong drink and women of easy virture...

Not these two.

Closer observation would reveal these men for what they actually were. Filling their saddles were a pair of gunfighters, men who had looked death squarely in the eye, yet lived to see another sunrise. These were men who had given birth to legend; stories told and retold, exploits which grew larger with each telling.

The riders were not reckless men, foolish souls who charged into battle without any consideration of life or limb. They each understood the dangers they faced and were closely familiar with the consequences of their failure. Fear was not a condition foreign to them, but they hadn't bowed their knees to its threat. The fact of their existence was a tribute to their dogged tenacity and will to survive—and their obvious skills with a gun.

These were men whose nostrils were filled with the scent of ancient gun smoke. Their ears rang with the echoes of exploding gunfire and the cries of the fallen. Their eyes and minds gave witness to the men they left dead, face down in dusty, wind-blown city streets and bluish smoke-filled saloons. When the guns were still, when the night wind blew cool off the mountains, and when the crickets sang, only then did the memories haunt them.

One of the pair sold his gun to the highest bidder, a soldier of fortune, unconcerned about the right or wrong of an issue. Joe Clements' loyalty was often limited by the challenge of the job and the size of the employer's bank account.

The other traveler, equally as fast, only drew a gun in defense of himself or others. Kellen Malone had never allowed his gun or his loyalties to be purchased.

Two such men would never meet, unless it was over drawn six-guns in a dusty street. Stranger still, the two were seen riding together, exchanging pleasantries. That in itself was reason enough for curiosity and suspicion.

Sitting in a chair, leaning on two legs against the wall of the eating house, a gray-haired, elderly gentleman contentedly whittled on a piece of wood. The old man's face was pale and haggard, eyes sunk deeply into his head. He stopped whittling occasionally to send a stream of tobacco juice in the direction of the brass spittoon resting beside him. The stains on the floor bore witness to his accuracy, or rather his lack of it.

Whittling was the old man's sport of choice. It gave him a chance to ponder life's great mysteries and to reminisce about younger, better days. He enjoyed the glow of the sunshine, as its rays warmed his weary bones. Nothing constructive or artistic was ever produced by his activity. No beautiful wooden figurines ever came forth as wood gave way to steel. It was just something he did to pass the time. But most of all, whittling in this place gave him the opportunity to be the first person to see strangers drifting into Redhawk.

The old man looked up suddenly as the two riders walked their horses up the street. He squinted to make out their faces, his wrinkled hand shielding his eyes from the sun. There was a quality about these men that immediately captured his attention, the way they moved, the way they sat a horse, and the way they carried themselves. Something in their manner spoke of quiet confidence, an ability to handle whatever life chose to steer their way. Some would call them dangerous men; most would simply leave them alone.

Upon seeing the two riders a young mother hurriedly ushered her two, wide-eyed children into the safety of a nearby hardware store. In a window across the street, the town gossip pushed the curtain to one side, as her pair of prying eyes studied the two strangers. The curtain stayed to one side for a couple of minutes and then fell back into place as the horsemen passed her view. None of these things escaped the riders' attention, their senses honed keenly, missing not one detail of their surroundings.

The sudden flurry of activity brought a bitter scowl to the old man's face, his concentration on the pair broken. Then resuming his whittling, he continued to give them a careful appraisal.

The rider passing nearest to the old man's chair tipped his hat and spoke softly. "Howdy, old timer," he said, smiling.

The grizzled old man lifted his head, his eyes meeting those of the speaker. Wide-eyed, he took note of the stranger's face and the small, skull-shaped scar. Having heard only the man's description, he recognized the rider instantly. Upon seeing the face of the other horseman, an icy chill crept up and down his tired bones.

One of the faces rekindled a memory, a face known well to him—a friend. The other was a killer for hire, his face known only by description. When either of these two men rode into a town, the old man thought, trouble is usually riding at their side. But both of them together? Indeed, death had come to Redhawk!

"Morning, Jube," Malone said as he rode up beside him. "It's been a long time."

Momentarily speechless, the old man was surprised to see his friend alive. He finally found his tongue. "We all heard you were dead."

Malone drew rein next to the board sidewalk. Joe Clements stopped his horse beside him.

"You're the second person to tell me that, Jube. I'm beginning to wonder if it isn't just wishful thinking."

"No, no, Kell. Nothing like that. I'm just so glad to see you, boy! Really I am."

Malone just smiled. "Still busy at your whittling, I see. Ever learn to make anything yet?"

"No, Kell. Just frittering away the afternoon."

While taking in the conversation, Joe rested his horse. He leaned forward, his arms crossed on the saddle horn.

"Knew a man one time who used to whittle toy soldiers out of wood. Pretty good at it too."

"I never learned to carve no soldiers," the old man replied, smiling slightly. "Or anything else for that matter."

"Well, you're still young yet," Kell said with a grin. "See you around, Jube."

"See you, Kell. And welcome back!"

Malone started up the street with Clements trailing along beside.

In his haste to spread the news to the sheriff, the old man dropped his knife. Reaching down to pick it up, the chair fell out from underneath him. Jubal sprawled onto the wooden planks. His cursing could be heard by folks from across the street.

The riders dismounted in front of the livery stable, watching with quiet amusement as the old man, running like a youngster, rushed off towards the sheriff's office.

"Who's the old codger?"

"Just a lonely, old man, someone I knew seven long years ago. Been whittling in that same spot for almost a decade now," Malone explained. "Ever since his wife died." A lump came to Kell's throat, his thoughts returning to Alice. He quickly changed the subject. "Are you going to buy me that drink now, Joe, or do I have to die of thirst?"

"I thought you were buying."

"Me?"

"Seems like the least you can do, me supplying the water canteen and all."

"Reckon you've got me there." Malone smiled. "I was hoping you forgot about that."

"I never forget a debt."

The hostler met them at the door and they handed over the reins. "Take good care of these horses for us," Kell said, "Be sure they get a good measure of oats. They sure earned it. We'll settle up with you later."

"Malone started towards the saloon, while Joe got the rifle from off his saddle's scabbard. "You coming, Joe? Haven't changed your mind about the beer, have you?"

"I'm right behind you, Malone. Be sure you don't stop quick or I'll leave boot tracks up your back."

Redhawk had one saloon within its borders, the Lady Luck. It was a tiny, insignificant place, one whose meager and common appearance belied it considerable profits. Situated in the center of town, not only in location, but also in importance, the Lady Luck was always brimming full of customers.

Men came within its walls for any number of reasons; to make cattle deals, where a handshake counted more than a lawyer's legal papers; to glean information on a new trail westward; or simply to pass the time of day. Some came to give away their hard-earned dollars at a poker table, swelling the pockets of cheats or better players. Most common of all, they came to wet down their thirsts.

The Lady Luck always held a special fondness for Kell, since it was the only establishment in town not owned by Clay Adkins. The bartender and proprietor was a heavy-set fellow, who answered to the name of Buck Halstead.

Halstead and Malone went back a number of years together, in other states, other towns. Buck had even worked for Kell at one time, as a deputy in a small, Kansas cow town. He'd been a good one too, until he lost his nerve. It happens to a man sometimes, looking down too many barrels while upholding the law he's sworn to enforce. Finally, Buck had enough. He gave up his guns and badge, drew his pay, and lit out for parts unknown.

Years later, while drifting whichever way his horse's nose was pointed, Kell drew rein outside the Lady Luck. To his surprise, there was Halstead behind the bar. He looked the same as Malone remembered, except for being a few years older and several pounds heavier. Happy as he was to cross the path of an old friend, Buck had little to do with Kell's decision to settle in Redhawk.

Buck Halstead didn't live alone . . .

Out back of the saloon, Buck shared a small place with his kid sister, Alice. She was a lovely girl of sweet disposition, with auburn hair and green eyes. The last time Kell had seen her, she was nothing more than a wide-eyed, skinny kid, way too small for the keeping—the kind to be taken off the hook and tossed back into the stream.

Kell quickly determined that the years had been kind to Alice. She had grown taller and more attractive, filling out her clothes in all the ways a woman should. Her smile shined so brightly that it made the sun jealous enough to wrap itself in a cloud to hide its shame.

A beautiful girl living that closely to the saloon did nothing to harm Buck's profits. Men would ride for sixty miles just to catch a glimpse of her and twice that distance for a smile. Alice Halstead certainly had no shortage of willing suitors. Like so many others, Kellen Malone was smitten with just one look. But Kell was the lucky one, the man who would make Alice Halstead his wife.

Yet Alice was not the only thing that Malone and Halstead had in common. In addition to Jesse, Kell's son, they had each developed a mutual hatred and general distrust for Clay Adkins.

***

Joe Clements paused outside the swinging doors of the Lady Luck. Kell watched with interest as Clements loosed the gun in his holster before entering. It was a habit of Malone's also, a liability of the lives they led—and a necessity of their continued survival.

Those who lived by the gun could never be free of it. Too many had fallen by their hand; too many of their relatives thirsted to even the score. Then there were the younger ones, the fools. These were the reckless and eager, searching for fame and recognition, purchased at the expense of blood.

Stopping just inside the doors, Kell let his eyes adjust to the change in lighting, another necessary habit he had acquired. As his vision returned, Kell was taken with the things he saw there. Men were standing at the bar, some seated at tables, free, doing whatever they wished. Malone had seen little of that in seven years.

The saloon's high pitched ceiling echoed with the sounds of conversation and laughter. The clinking of bottles and glasses could be heard also. A cloud of bluish smoke hovered in the air, suspended just about eye level.

Malone and Clements weaved their way through the crowd. They chose an empty place among the patrons at the bar. A pair of hard-cases looked up from their drinks, and then disregarded them, seemingly uninterested in another pair of footloose drifters.

Giving more attention to the mahogany than the customers, Buck Halstead was polishing the bar with a rag.

"We'll have a couple of beers," Kell said, a wry smile on his lips.

Halstead never looked up. He simply wiped his hands on his apron, mumbling something as he went to fetch their drinks. He placed them on the bar in front of Malone and Clements, never once meeting their gaze.

"How much do I owe you, Barkeep?"

"Why that'll be . . ." Then he lifted his eyes. A look of startled recognition came to his face, followed by silence. It was a characteristic unknown to the burly barkeeper. He looked like someone who had just seen a ghost. Halstead thought he just did.

"Kell!" he exclaimed. "Kellen Malone! How are you doing, boy? We thought you were dead."

The normal sounds of the saloon immediately became a near-deafening silence, as all eyes turned in their direction. Many of the faces were familiar to Malone, some of them old friends. Others carried expressions of shock, curiosity, suspicion, and even resentment. The silence soon gave way to quiet murmurs, growing louder as the seconds passed. Some quickly got up to leave.

"Don't pay them no mind, Kell!" Buck bellowed loud enough for all to hear. "They can't help being stupid."

Kell and Joe tossed down their drinks.

"Okay, what's the story, Kell? They brought a body into town the other day, just about your size," Halstead explained. "Pretty bad shape it was! Scalped, mutilated . . . you know the Apaches. Men said they found it between here and Yuma prison. We all figured it was you."

"Don't look so disappointed, Buck. There's always next time," Kell replied, smiling. He then turned serious. "What made you think it was me?"

"This," Buck said, reaching his hand under the bar. He then came out with a bullet-ridden canteen, placing it in front of Malone. "Remember the horse and outfit I had waiting for you at the prison?"

"Yea, Buck. Don't know how I can thank you." Malone looked puzzled. "But what's that got to do with everyone thinking I'm dead?"

"The canteen, Kell. Look at it closely."

Malone emptied the now-useless canteen, for the first time seeing the inscription on the side. Clements looked over his shoulder as Kell read the words. He swallowed hard at the inscription:

"Kellen Malone—A Free Man"

Although he'd never been known as the sentimental type, Kell was genuinely touched by the gift from his brother-in-law. "Lot of good it will do me, all full of holes," he muttered, all the while maintaining his tough facade.

Halstead's wide, always smiling face was now doing his best wounded puppy imitation. Although he tried to keep a straight face, the laugh wrinkles around his eyes made it difficult to pull off. "I just don't know what to say. I'm really hurt. Man gives you a fancy gift, Kell, you ought to take better care of it."

Malone laughed. "As I recall, I was a mite busy at the time."

"I can vouch for that," offered Joe. "He was surrounded by Apaches when I showed up. There was Running Hawk and some of Geronimo's bunch. Probably a dozen, all told. They almost got me too."

"I don't believe that!" shouted a voice from the crowd.

The speaker was a young man with wolfish eyes and shoulder length, blond hair that had never been touched with a comb. He stood to his feet quickly, his blue eyes glistening with the anticipation of trouble and the opportunity to kill. His name was Yance, a cousin of the famous gunman, Tom Candrey.

"A man surrounded by that many Apaches don't live to talk about it," he said, hoping to push Malone into a fight.

Malone turned at the sound of the challenge. Clements restrained him with a hand to his chest. "Allow me," Joe said.

Clements walked over to the stranger, a grin on his face and malice in his soul. In his right hand, Joe still held the half-full beer mug. "I wouldn't like it if you're calling my friend a liar. Like it even less if you're calling me one. Which one is it, Long Hair?"

Upon learning he must face this stranger, the blond gunman's heart leaped. After dispensing with this one, he figured to kill Malone—two for the price of one. Then he saw the skull-shaped scar on the man's cheek. Candrey needed no further introductions. At the realization he was facing Skull Clements, Yance's face turned ashen.

"Which is it, long hair!" Clements was merciless. "You calling me or my friend a liar?"

Candrey noticed the beer mug filling Joe's gun hand, knowing that Skull must drop it before drawing. The longer he looked, the better he liked his chances. His fingers began to twitch above his pistol butt. Yance knew he could beat this man, the vanity of youth casting aside his limited good sense.

Yance craved the reputation his cousin, Tom, had achieved, the notoriety of being known as handy with a gun. Although Tom Candrey had chosen not to exploit his fame, he hungered after the status that fame would earn him. He saw the way people stepped aside whenever Wes Hardin entered a room. Yance wanted that. Killing Skull Clements is all it would take to make a man into a legend.

Clements continued to push hard, refusing to let up on the young man. "Say something, Long Hair! Cat got your tongue?"

Candrey took a long, hard look into Clement's green eyes, cold as an emerald in a blizzard. He could see no fear in them . . . only death. Swallowing hard, he decided the reputation wasn't worth the cost.

"I reckon I spoke out of turn, mister." The words nearly caught in his throat. Yance Candrey eased his hand away from his gun. Then, hanging his head in shame, he quietly slipped out of the saloon.

Clements watched the young man until he was gone from the saloon. Then he drank down the last of his beer and made his way back to the bar.

"You just made an enemy," Malone said quietly.

"Yeah," Clements muttered, as he finished sipping his beer. "So what?"

"You know he'll try to kill you for that, don't you, Joe?"

"Well, the line forms at the rear."

"With Candrey," Buck observed, "that's the end you better watch."

Kell and Joe laughed at the bartender's remark.

Buck continued his conversation as if nothing had ever happened. "Anyway, that's why we thought the body was yours, Kell. Someone found the canteen."

"It's likely the dead man's name was Dotson," Kell explained. "He used to be a guard at the prison. Had a couple of run-ins with the guy. Thought he had a score to settle. As it turned out, the Apaches never gave him a chance." Malone smiled at the bartender. "You never did tell me what I owe you for these drinks."

"You know your money is no good in my place. Not today! Besides, I'm just glad you're alive."

"At least let me buy one for my friend."

"Nothing doing! Any friend of yours is welcomed here."

"Excuse me for my manners," Kell said. "Buck Halstead, I want you to meet the man who put Yance Candrey to flight."

"We've already met. Good to see you again, Joe."

"Same here," Clements said with a smile.

"You boys look like you're still thirsty," Buck said, taking their mugs to refill them.

Malone's face turned serious. "Buck, where's Jesse?"

"Did you try the school house?" Halstead looked up from getting their beers. "He ought to be there now, although I haven't seen him for a couple days." Buck returned to his place at the bar, setting the drinks in front of the pair. "And these two are also on the house, gents."

Clements looked sheepish. "If you fellows will excuse me, it looks like you want to talk in private. Thanks for the brews."

"Okay, Joe," Buck said.

"See you around later," Kell added.

Joe nodded while lifting his beer. He started for a table in the back of the saloon.

"Did Jesse think I was dead too, Buck?"

Halstead nodded. "Everybody did."

"How did he take it?"

The bartender hesitated before answering. "Like everyone else, I guess. Didn't really say much . . . but who really knows much about kids."

Malone had known the bartender for years. Kell had never known the man to be a good liar. He could sense that Buck was hiding something—holding something back.

"Level with me, Buck. What aren't you saying?"

"Some things are better left unsaid."

"Look, Buck. I just spent seven years paying for something I didn't do. My wife, your sister, died while I was in prison. I lost everything, including my reputation. After all that, what could you possibly say that would hurt me?"

"Jesse said he was glad you were dead." Halstead was ashamed of the brutal way he spat out the words.

Malone hung his head, trying to digest this latest information. He said nothing for a time, before finally lifting his head. Halstead could see the pain in his eyes.

"Why isn't Jesse staying with you, Buck?"

Halstead's face grew red and the veins swelled in his neck. "You can blame Adkins for that, him and that lawyer, Carlton Stadler. They said I'd be an unfit example, with me being a bartender and living out back of the saloon. They even got some crooked judge to back them up."

Buck returned to polishing the bar as Malone returned to his drink. His mind was on Jesse. Just then, the doors swung open. Kell threw an uninterested look in their direction. He suddenly found himself staring at a familiar face, a man he hated . . .

Clay Adkins.

As their eyes met, Clay stopped in his tracks. There was surprise and disbelief in his eyes. It lasted for but a second. His darting, snake-like eyes changed their expression as easily as a chameleon changes colors.

In their place, Malone saw a taunting, self-assured gleam, a look of smugness which quickly rekindled the contempt Kell held for him.

"Kellen Malone," he said loudly, for all in the room to hear, "the reports of your death must have been incorrect. You're looking well." The tone was mocking.

Leaving his beer only half finished, Kell made his way over to the man. As he approached Adkins, the two men who followed him stepped forward. Menacingly, they took positions to the left and right behind Clay.

Deke and Sam Hinton were a couple of never-do-wells, men who built their reputation in a Waco saloon, killing four drunken cowboys. There had been other murders along the way, ambushes, stage robberies, and the like.

Deke was a belligerent man of average height and below average intelligence. His manner of speech ran parallel to the thoughts in his mind, slow and garbled. When he spoke, the words were mumbled and sometimes unintelligible. But the gun he carried spoke loud, clear, and often.

Sam Hinton's intelligence only rated a playing card thickness above his brother's. Walking with a limp, Sam was a portrait of disarray. His boots were run down at the heel, his jeans worn out in the seat. His toes pointed in and his knees bowed out. Only his gun hung straight.

Ignoring the outlaws who protected him, Malone stared Clay in the eyes. "You look like a man who's roped and thrown the world and bound its legs in a piggin' string. Everything going to suit you, Clay?"

"I can't complain."

"Want us to handle him?" Deke mumbled, as he started to step forward. His eyes were eager.

Clay restrained him. "No, Deke. Let the man have his say. Words can do us no harm."

"I want to know where Jesse is, Clay." The remark was calm and patient; Kell was not.

"He doesn't want to see you, Malone." Clay's eyes danced in triumph. "He was better off thinking you were dead. The boy curses the ground you crawl on. In fact, he clearly blames you for his mother's death."

"I want to see him!"

"No!"

That's for him to decide, Clay, not the likes of you."

"First, you shamed your wife and now you want to drag your boy through the same hog wallow. I won't let you, Malone. Jesse belongs to me now."

Malone's eyes turned cold and deadly. "I ought to kill you for that, Clay! I ought to kill you right here and now."

Clay smiled, deliberately taunting the man again. "By the way, whatever happened to the bandits who rode with you?"

At that moment, Deke Hinton went for his gun . . .

Moving with a speed seldom seen in the West, Kell drew with both hands. Both guns came level before Deke ever cleared leather. Hinton froze with his gun only half way out of the holster. He braced for a bullet that never came.

"Leave it holstered, Deke! Same goes for you too." Kell stepped forward and hammered Deke Hinton with his pistol barrel, sending the man reeling to the floor. His other gun covered Sam and Clay.

"Why don't you just shuck that pistol, Sam! I'll even give you a chance," he said, holstering his gun. "It's more than you and your brother gave those drunken cowboys in Waco."

"You can take him," Clay said.

"Yeah, Sam. Listen to him and you'll be dead." The tone of Kell's voice took a sharp edge. "You either grab iron or drag your brother out of here to see the doc. Those are your only choices."

Hinton, suddenly realizing how close he was to death, didn't take long in making up his mind. Sam bent over and helped his scarcely conscious brother to his feet. Together, the pair moved slowly through the swinging doors.

Clay watched them go and then shot Kell a hard look. "You should have killed them while you had the chance, Malone. It's clear to me that you learned nothing in prison. You're still a fool! Now they'll kill you and you won't even see it coming." Adkins paused. "And if you weren't wearing those guns, I'd kill you myself . . . with my bare hands."

"How about now?" Kell unbuckled his twin six-guns, walked over, and handed them across the counter to Buck Halstead "Hold these for a minute."

The room grew as quiet as a funeral parlor as Clay removed his holster as well.

"Roll up your sleeves, Adkins, and take your best shot."

This moment was Malone's first real look at Clay Adkins. The man looked like a huge wall of granite, towering four inches about Kell's six-foot stature.

Clay grinned viciously and licked his lips, still not believing anyone would have the nerve to challenge him. Adkins had crushed men before—in business and in battle. Some said that Clay had killed a man with his bare hands once, snapping the man's spine like a dry twig. Standing there before him, Kell believed the stories.

Malone swung first . . .

A work-hardened, calloused right hand landed squarely against Clay's jaw. The punch left nothing but a smile on Adkins' face. Kell cursed softly, knowing he'd just tackled a tornado.

Clay threw a hulking a right hand at Malone, thrown with all the force of his bulk. Kell ducked underneath the punch. If it had landed, the fight would have been a short one. Kell smiled at his good fortune and his punch stabbed Adkins in the wind.

The assault only halted him momentarily. Clay then rushed Malone, hitting him like a buffalo stampede. The two men crashed into the table. The legs gave way, breaking bottles and spilling whiskey on the floor.

They came to their feet quickly and Kell connected with a left and a right to the nose. Clay was knocked off balance, but quickly recovered. Then he backhanded Malone alongside the skull.

It was a crushing blow, one that sent the smaller man flying like a rag doll in a windstorm. Kell hit the floor in a heap and rolled against the bar. Clay rushed forward, booting him twice in the ribs, the kicks lifting his body off the floor. The pain was shooting all through him. Catching Adkins' leg, Malone thrust him off. Clay was staggered as Kell came to his feet.

One of the saloon's patrons started inching a hand towards his gun. Joe Clements stared at him coldly, with his gun pointed. "Let them fight," he said.

Halstead pulled a shotgun and scanned the room for anybody else who might want to buy chips in this game.

Kell feinted with a right, then rifled a left to Clay's teeth. His knuckles turned red as they split Clay's mouth. Two more combinations to his belly and a right to the eye sent Adkins tumbling into the bar. Clay threw a nearly-full whiskey bottle at Malone, but Kell managed to duck underneath it. Then he was all over Malone again.

Still grinning through bloody teeth, Adkins showed no signs of tiring. His punches jarred Kell to the bone. Malone circled him warily, looking for an opening. For a big man, Clay was surprisingly fast and agile.

Malone threw another jab his way and the big man took it coming in. Clay merely shook his head and laughed out loud at the blow. Two massive hands raised Kell's feet off the floor. Adkins pinned the smaller adversary against bar, trying to crush his spine on the edge of the mahogany.

"I got you now," he said, smiling.

Flaming arrows of pain shot all through him. Malone could feel his hands and feet growing numb. Throwing his head forward, Kell savagely butted him in the face, loosing the man's grip. Clay grunted like a wounded animal, his nose broken. The blood flowed dark and heavy from above his mouth.

Now free, Kell hammered him with a couple of rights, driving the big man backwards. They stood in the middle of the saloon, toe to toe, trading punches. They matched each other, blow for blow, the fists landing like thrusts from a sledgehammer.

Clay, the bigger man, was now tiring quickly. Kell could sense it. At the same time, he realized that he didn't have much more left in him either. Kell knew he had to end it soon!

A pair of stinging left hands made Adkins stagger stupidly, blows that would have downed most men. Stubbornly, the man swayed, but remained on his feet.

Most of Clay's punches found no target. Those that landed had no sting. His breath was coming in hoarse gasps. He continued to stand, driven by a savage desire to win, to destroy.

Summoning his last ounce of strength, Kell put everything he had into a final, overhand right . . .

The blow landed squarely on Adkins' upturned nose, with the entire force of Kell's body behind it. Clay just stood there, his nose cocked at a strange angle, with a befuddled look on his face.

Just as Kell wound up for another, Clay's knees buckled, and he pitched over on his face.

Battered and bloodied, Malone stood in the middle of the saloon, his shirt hanging in threads. The unconscious body of Clay rested at his feet. His knuckles were sore, hands swollen. Yet he didn't feel much like rejoicing over his victory. Kell ripped away his tattered shirt, standing there bare-chested. He tossed the scraps of fabric on Clay's head.

Joe took a bottle and poured Kell a shot of whiskey. "You look like you could use this, Malone."

"Thanks," he said, before downing it in one swallow. He then found his six-guns and slung them around his hips, buckling them into place.

By this time, Sheriff Bill Kimball made his way over to the saloon. "What's going on here?" he bellowed. Then he saw Kell. "Malone?"

Old Jubal had rushed over to tell Kimball that Kellen Malone and Joe Clements had just ridden into town. Despite that information, the sheriff still could not believe it was actually him—and that the man was still alive.

One of Clay's ranch hands, the one who tried pulling a gun earlier, had been playing cards at one of the tables when the fight started. "Malone started the whole thing," he said. "He threw the first punch, Sheriff."

"Is that true, Malone?"

"Lucky I didn't kill him. Yeah, Bill, I owed him that much. I kind of enjoyed it too."

Several snickers could be heard at the remark. The faces all turned somber when Kimball's scowl singled them out.

Bill's face turned a deep shade of red. "How would you enjoy spending the night in jail?"

"Probably a lot less than I liked this," Kell said, grinning.

"Come on now, Marshal," Halstead interrupted. "You know Clay had it coming."

"You stay out of this, Buck!" Then turning towards Kell, Kimball replied, "And you better get out of my sight, Malone, before I run you in."

"Okay, Bill. But I won't drop this until I find Jesse."

"He ought to be in school now, but you can see him when it lets out. That should give you plenty of time to get a new shirt, maybe clean yourself up some."

"Thanks, Bill," he muttered, finding his hat on the floor.

Halstead smiled as Kell slung the bullet-scarred canteen over his bare shoulder.

Then the sheriff caught Joe Clements' eye. "I heard you were in town, Skull. Don't you start no trouble in Redhawk! There's no paper on you right now, so I can't arrest you. But if you so much as look cross-eyed at one of our citizens, or pull a gun on one of them, then I'll see that they lynch you with your own gunbelt. You understand me, mister?"

Joe just grinned. "Okay, Sheriff. I wouldn't want that."

Buck and Joe waved to Kell as he left the saloon.

"Kell!" Kimball shouted behind him, stopping the man in mid-stride. "I'm glad you ain't dead."

"That makes two of us, Bill."

Chapter Six

After Malone left the saloon, Clay Adkins regained consciousness, bitterly flinging the tattered shirt off his head. He buckled on his gun and dusted the sawdust from his clothes. Grabbing a towel off the bar, Clay wiped the blood and sweat from his face before ordering a drink.

Buck poured him a glass of whiskey, smiling as he did so. "You don't look so good, Clay."

"Just shut up and leave the bottle, Halstead!"

Bottle and glass in hand, Clay chose a table in the back, away from the other customers. Still carrying his beer, Clements joined him.

"That was quite a scrap between you boys," Joe said. "Glad I got to see it. You two must be really old friends."

Adkins looked disgusted, wiping away the remainder of the blood with a whiskey-dampened handkerchief from his pocket. He winced at the pain.

"Why didn't you help?"

"Malone was doing fine without me," Clements shot back, making no effort to restrain his laughter.

Adkins jumped from his seat, his face twisted in rage, fingers near the butt of his gun. "No one makes fun of me, Clements! Not you . . . not anyone!"

Many of the saloon's customers raced from the door, contented that they had already witnessed enough violence for one day. And many of them were not anxious to risk getting caught up in any more.

Joe made no effort to move or go for his gun. He continued to sit there, coldly distant, bored, like a rattler sunning himself on a rock. These were the moments when Joe Clements was the most deadly, a serpent ready to bare its fangs if threatened.

Adkins saw something in the gunman's green eyes which warned him of the danger he faced. Allowing his better judgment to guide his actions, Clay eased his hand away from the gun. No sooner had that been done, Clements returned to his normal, easy-going manner.

"I asked you before, Skull. Why didn't you do anything to help me?"

"It wasn't my fight."

"I'm not paying you to sit and watch me take a beating."

"You're not paying me anything at all, yet. I just rode into town and I haven't seen the color of your money." Joe took a long pull from his beer. "And let me tell you something else. You take a lot of chances, Clay . . . a lot of chances. Dead men ain't much count at paying up."

"I've reserved you a room at the hotel," Adkins explained, barely above a whisper. "You take that room. Underneath a loose floorboard, you'll find five thousand dollars in cash."

"Five thousand bucks will buy a man a lot of help," Joe remarked. "A lot of help."

"And I expect you to earn every penny of it. Top wages demand top performance. If my other men fail in their attempt, then the job will fall to you."

"And if they succeed?"

"Then I will have something else for you to do. Either way," Adkins said, tossing down his drink, "you'll earn your money."

"Sounds easy enough, so far. What's the job?"

Adkins leaned over to Clements and whispered softly, "Skull, I want Kellen Malone dead."

Clements cocked an eyebrow. So that was it. Joe remembered the conversation he'd had with Malone earlier, after leaving the ranch. Malone said he wouldn't like the work, Clements recalled. So, Kell had already guessed Clay's intentions. More and more, Joe found himself admiring Malone's guts and savvy.

It took courage to ride with a man who would soon be gunning for you. He wondered why Malone hadn't just shot him on the way to town. No doubt there had been plenty of opportunities. Joe didn't need to ponder over an answer. Malone, like himself, would only shoot a man who was facing him. There weren't many of those left, Joe thought.

Sam Hinton and the Mexican named Julio entered the saloon and joined them at the table. Joe looked the pair over with knowing eyes, immediately recognizing the Mexican as the better of the two. He had already seen Sam in action.

"If you got any plans to tackle Kellen Malone, I wouldn't try it with this outfit." Clements sneered at the two men who had joined them at the table. "These two wouldn't make a patch on a real bad man!" He smiled suddenly. "Hey, Sam. How's your brother's sore head doing?"

The two men stared at Clements coldly, hatred filling their eyes. "I think maybe I cut you, Senor," Julio said bitterly.

Clements pointed at the scar on his cheek. "It's been tried before, Mex. You ought to see the other guy. They buried him the next day. It seems the undertaker had to clean him up first."

Adkins grew impatient. "I want an answer, Skull. Will you take the job?"

"I'll think on it."

"Are you afraid of him?" The words slipped out before Clay could catch himself. He knew how the remark would be taken and Adkins found himself wanting to find a place to hide from the reaction.

Joe's eyes turned cold once again. "No, I'm not afraid of Malone, but I'm not stupid either. The man's good. He's deadly. And he saved my life once. No, make that a couple of times.

"Something else you ought to know . . . about Malone being hard to kill, I mean. We rode in together, him and me. Along the way, we had a bad scrape with the Apaches. Worst of it took place before I got there. Malone killed at least six. And Running Hawk was one of them.

"It must have been quite a tussle, hand-to-hand and all. Would have give anything to seen it!" Clements stared hard at Adkins. "Don't underestimate the man. Ones like him don't kill easy."

"Okay, Skull. The job has been offered. Take it or get out of town," Clay explained, his courage somewhat lifted by the presence of the others. "If you stay in town, you work for me . . . or I figure you're working for him. And one other thing. I hate loose ends. You have until tomorrow to give me an answer."

"Sounds fair enough, Clay."

Joe finished his beer and went to the bar for another. Clay and his men remained at the back table, seemingly in no hurry to leave.

Clements stood next to the bar. He sipped his beer slowly and mulled over the job offer made by Adkins. It was a fair amount for a man's life, better than many of the jobs he had taken. But still, Malone wouldn't be easy, he thought. And worst of all, he felt he owed Kell a debt.

Obligations were things he had a hard time forgetting. Joe downed the last of his beer and decided to sleep on the decision. A room at the hotel and a soft, warm bed—the idea sounded good to him.

From his place at the end of the bar, Montana Hodges had been watching their meeting with interest. Joe left the saloon, as Montana's eyes followed him. Hodges lingered over his beer for a time, then made his way outside.

***

After the fight in the saloon, Malone went to the general store to purchase a new shirt. Kell chose the one he wanted and flipped a gold piece on the counter. The storekeeper tossed it right back to him.

"Malone, I hear you just beat the stuffing out of Clay Adkins. Is that true?"

"I guess news travels fast."

"I'd give my right arm just to have seen it. Just hearing about it makes it worth the price of a shirt."

"Well, thanks for your kindness," Malone said, smiling.

"No! Thank you, Kellen Malone. Years ago, I ran beef on a ranch west of here," the man said. "You hauled water into town during the drought. Saved my herd and a lot of others. I always did want to thank you, personal like. Sorry it was so long in coming."

"How are your beeves doing now?"

"Probably been eat by now. Wife gave me an ultimatum . . . her or the cows. I thought on it for a long time, mind you." The storekeeper broke into a smile. "The beeves gave me less trouble, but I figured twenty years of marriage ought to be worth something. I sold every last one of them, right down to the hoof. Used the money to buy me this here store."

"It's none of my business, mister, but what have you got against Clay Adkins?"

"Adkins bought an interest in my store two years ago. Did the same with everyone in town, everyone but Halstead." The storekeeper checked the street. "He threatened my wife and kids if I didn't sell him a piece of the business. I hate the man!"

"What about Buck? Why didn't Clay force Halstead to sell?"

"Couple of reasons, I guess. Halstead don't have no family around here, so Adkins couldn't use that for leverage. But mostly, Clay is afraid to try."

"Afraid? Afraid of what?"

"The whole town, Malone. Redhawk only has one saloon in town and Buck's the only barkeep. If anything happened to either one, then men in town are liable to get stirred up. Hard to tell whose neck might get stretched."

Kell laughed out loud. "Thanks for the information. And once again, thank you for the shirt." Malone started towards the door.

"Kell, about the shirt . . ." he replied, stopping Kell in the doorway. "It's coming out of Clay's share of the profits."

Malone laughed all the way up the street.

Stopping at the water trough, Kell bathed the sweat and blood from his body. A buckboard came into town as he stood there. Malone paid it no mind, until he saw the woman driving. It was Rachel Payton.

Malone tipped his hat to her, but she made no response to his gesture, looking on him with disdain. Her eyes lingered on the man for a time as she continued onward. The smell of lilacs hung in the air. Kell returned to his bathing, his lips whistling a tune. He then slipped into the fresh, clean shirt.

Using the surface of the water as a mirror, Kell smoothed down his hair. He winced while shoving the hat back on his sore head. Clay hit hard; Malone had to give him that. His mind then turned to filling his belly.

On the other side of the street, with a mile-wide grin, there stood his friend, Montana Hodges.

Malone walked up to him and pumped his hand. "It's good to see you again, Montana. How are you?"

"Couldn't be better. It's been a long time, Kell."

"Too long."

Hodges noticed the bullet-scarred canteen slung over his shoulder. "What's that?"

"Just a little gift from a friend."

"A canteen that leaks. Maybe you ought to cultivate some new friends."

Kell laughed. "Guess that says something about my choice of friends."

The two men started walking together towards the livery stable, where Malone checked on his horse. Kell left the canteen with his other gear, but not without a strange look from the hostler. Malone fumbled in his pocket for some money and then paid the boy.

"That reminds me," Hodges said, reaching deep into his pocket. Out he came with five, twenty-dollar gold pieces. "These are yours."

Kell held out his hand. "What are these for?"

Montana gave a strange laugh. "Guess you have been gone for a long time, Kell. Most folks use them for money." His face quickly turned serious. "Alice always kept some money in a box above the mantle. Saved it up, I guess. You were a lucky man, Kell. Her last thoughts were of you. Alice said something about giving these to you when you got back."

Malone looked puzzled. "Why did she give them to you instead of her brother, Buck?"

"I don't have a clue, Kell. And does it really matter? At least you got them."

"I guess you're right, Montana." He shook the money in his hand before sticking it in his pocket. "Alice always did spend her time worrying about everyone else." Kell swallowed hard. "It might have been the thing that killed her. The woman never drew a selfish breath."

Hodges nodded.

Malone felt a need to quickly change the subject. "I don't know about you, Montana, but I'm needing to put on the feed bag. "Care to tag along? Give us a chance to catch up on old times."

"Only if you let me buy."

"I reckon there has to be a first time for everything," Kell joked. "Follow me."

As they made their way down the street, Malone saw a man duck quickly into the alley. Limping as he was, Kell figured the man to be

Sam Hinton. He shook his head. Over the years, Kell had seen many plays like this or ones similar. At that moment, he wished his hands weren't quite so swollen from the fight.

Montana was walking behind him, so he had no way of knowing if his friend was aware of their impending danger. Kell couldn't risk turning his head or looking away.

"Heads up, Montana," he said softly.

"I saw him," Montana replied.

Kell continued walking towards the diner, conscious of every detail. Twenty yards in front of the building, a man sprang from the shadows. His gun blazing before he stepped into the open, a couple of bullets whipped past Malone as he drew.

Coolly, Kell leveled his gun and fired. Only one shot was needed. The man was spun around from the force of the bullet and slumped against the side of the wall. As his life's blood flowed away, the stranger whispered something about his mother.

From the upstairs window of the hotel, Sam Hinton took up slack in the trigger. Kell saw the flash of light reflected off the barrel. Instinctively, he crouched lower and swung his gun upward to meet the challenge. His two shots sounded as one.

Sam stood in front of the window, smiling over his apparent victory. Suddenly, his fingers began to grow numb and the rifle became heavy. No longer able to hold it, the Winchester fell from his hands. Hinton staggered forward and tumbled through the open window. His body rolled down the roof, then landed with a thud in the street.

At the first sound of shooting, a crowd of people came hurrying down the street, the sheriff leading the charge. They gathered around the bodies like beggars at a feast.

Malone pushed through the crowd and rushed to Hinton's side. As he knelt beside the wounded outlaw, Kell knew he could do nothing.

Hinton had been gut shot. Between coughs, Sam tried to say something, knowing his time was near.

Someone in the crowd offered Malone a canteen and he held it to the dying man's lips. Sam took a small drink, wincing from the pain as he swallowed. Montana walked up beside them.

The man's expression suddenly changed, his eyes going from Malone to Hodges. "Why did you do it?" he asked. "We had him. Why?"

Those were the last words he would ever speak. Sam's body trembled violently. Then he was gone.

Kell looked at Hodges. "Could you make any sense of that?"

Montana shrugged. "He was in a lot of pain there. Might have been out of his head."

Kimball elbowed his way through the onlookers. "Some of you men take these bodies to the undertaker." He shot Malone a hard look. "There's been nothing but trouble since your return. If I had anything to hold you for, Kell, you'd be sitting behind bars right now."

"But they fired first, Bill. I just defended myself," Malone said, thumbing fresh shells into his gun.

"A couple of folks already told me that. Their testimony is the only thing keeping you out of my jail." The sheriff rubbed his eyes, looking much older than the summers he'd seen. "If you'll just get out of town, Kell, maybe folks won't be so tempted to shoot you."

"I've seen plenty of folks killed on the trail, same as in town, Bill. Leaving town is no guarantee someone won't shoot at you."

"That isn't my worry. Just make sure you don't get yourself killed in my jurisdiction."

"Bill, you're all heart." Malone motioned at his friend. "Come on, Montana. You still owe me a meal."

As the two men walked towards the diner, Kell looked over at Hodges. "What happened back there?"

"What do you mean, Kell?"

"Your gun, Montana. Could have used a little help."

"Darn it, Kell. The gun got hung up in my holster. Embarrassed to admit it, but I forgot to take the thong off the hammer."

"Lucky they weren't shooting at you."

***

Rachel had tied her apron strings thousands of times before, yet today she found it difficult. Her mind was preoccupied with the stranger bathing at the water trough. What a strange man he is, Rachel thought.

As she drove the buckboard into town, his broad shoulders had been bare before her eyes. Although it embarrassed her to admit it, she had taken a long look at the man. And then she had taken a second. It was no way from a decent woman to think or behave. Clay was to be her husband. She knew him to be a good man, with dozens of fine qualities.

But what did she know of this drifter—this Kellen Malone? Many believed him to be a stage robber, a common thief. She doubted that seven short years could alter a man's nature or change his thoughts. Why should Malone be any exception?

As Rachel prepared a fresh pot of coffee, she wondered about the other stories she had heard. Some said Malone was innocent, wrongly convicted of another's crime. Mr. Hodges claimed that to be the case.

She knew Jesse Malone to be a fine boy, hardly the product of a criminal's upbringing. But perhaps Alice had been responsible for that part of the boy's nature. Many women were. Still, she wondered if leaves ever fell too far from the trees that shed them.

Rachel wondered why these things troubled her. Kellen Malone was not concern of hers.

Gunshots took her mind off the subject . . .

Rachel rushed to the window, but could see nothing from her vantage point. A crowd of people went scurrying up the street, in the direction of the gunshots. Several of the townsfolk passed in front of the window. None of them offered any information.

About ten minutes later, she saw a pair of men, Kellen Malone and Montana Hodges, walking towards the diner. She felt strangely relieved to see the mysterious stranger, who had just appeared at her door earlier today.

As Rachel went to the door, Malone entered the room. Standing face to face with the man, she suddenly went speechless. Kell found his own tongue missing, also.

The words didn't come easy to the woman. "What happened out there?" she finally asked.

"Shootin' trouble, ma'am," Montana replied. "Kell took care of it."

"Was anyone hurt?"

"No one was hurt," Kell mumbled. "But a couple of men are dead." He hesitated over an explanation, but no suitable one came to mind. "It was a fair shooting, ma'am." It was all he could think to say.

"Is that supposed to be some kind of a reasonable explanation, Kellen Malone?" Rachel was unconvinced. "It was a fair shooting—you say the words as if they justify everything."

"Well, what do you want me to say?"

"A pair of men lie dead in the street and you show absolutely no concern over it. What kind of man are you anyway? Have you no value for human life?"

"Yes, ma'am, I value human life a great deal. Mine, most of all! But back shooters or those who lie in wait to ambush you are scarcely to be considered human. And as to my concern over their lives, I have none."

Rachel said nothing, obviously angered by his answer.

Montana spoke up, hoping to relieve the tension. "Kellen Malone, I want you to meet Rachel Payton, the most handsome woman in Redhawk. Soon to be married."

She flushed slightly. "Why thank you, Mr. Hodges."

Kell looked at Rachel, then at his friend. "We've already met, Montana. We met at the ranch."

Hodges felt awkward and out of place, as if he'd just walked into the middle of an argument. Both parties were silent, their eyes throwing daggers at one another. He tried to change the subject. "How about something to eat, Miss Payton?

"Will he be eating too?" she asked Montana, barely looking at Kell.

Malone nodded.

"Have a seat. I'll go get your coffee right away, Mr. Hodges," she said, smiling. Kell didn't even get a smile from the disgruntled waitress. "Yours too, Mr. Malone." The words came out as little more than a grunt.

Grinning, Hodges watched her stomp off towards the kitchen. Then he sat down at the table with Malone. "You care to explain any of that to me, Kell?"

Malone's face turned grim. "No, Montana. I don't."

Conventional wisdom warned that Hodges shouldn't push the issue. But for a man who grew up poking sticks in hornets' nests, wisdom was not a virtue to generally be considered. Montana flashed his most devilish grin. "I think she's getting kind of sweet on you, Kell."

Malone glared at his friend silently. He could think of plenty of things to say, none of them pleasant. As he started to speak, the door swung open.

Frustrated and angry, his face red, Sheriff Kimball charged into the diner. Kimball was a heavy-set man, his voice usually low and deep.

When excited, the tone and pitch of his voice grew higher, becoming shrill enough to give a man a headache.

"Doggone you, Kell. I thought you were leaving town. The undertaker's already used twice as many coffins today as he used in the last three months. I can't have this."

Malone didn't let him finish. "Don't even say it, Bill." he bellowed. "I'll be out of town before nightfall."

"You'd darn well better be!" Kimball shuffled out the door, still muttering something about Redhawk used to be a quiet town. The door slammed behind him.

Malone looked over at Hodges, his face as solemn as a pallbearer. "You get the feeling he's upset?"

Montana laughed. "Don't ask me. I had my fingers in my ears the whole time."

As the two of them ate, Malone noticed Rachel standing in the kitchen doorway, throwing icy stares in his direction. He wondered what she must truly think of him."

Montana finished eating quickly, then got up to leave. "I've got some business in town. Later, Kell."

"See you around, Montana."

With Hodges gone, Rachel surrendered to her curiosity, making her way over to Malone's table. She stood there watching for several minutes, saying nothing. Malone didn't look up from his plate, figuring she'd get to the point eventually.

"A knife and a fork—who would ever believe it?" she blustered. "At least you don't eat like an animal too."

Malone looked up from his plate. "You know, lady, I've never been lauded for my mastery of the social graces before," he said, sarcastically. "You sound like a woman with something on her mind. Why don't you just have a seat and discuss it, Miss Payton? But then again, maybe you don't wish to be seen talking to the likes of me."

"I was just wondering what kind of man you are, Kellen Malone. Two men are dead and you sit here eating like nothing ever happened!" she exploded. "Why is that?"

"I guess I was hungry."

"You know what I mean!"

"Yes, Miss Payton, I'm afraid I do. Begging your pardon, ma'am. But I really don't think it's any of your affair."

Rachel momentarily stiffened at Kell's response, but she did her best to hide it. "I know it isn't any of my business, Mr. Malone. I'm just curious, that's all. At first glance, you appear to be a gentleman. I was just wondering how someone of your obviously fine upbringing could also be a killer."

Malone threw back his head and laughed. "What do you know of my upbringing, Miss Payton?"

"Nothing really," she said, bewildered by the humor that Malone found in her statement. "You just appear to be someone of high breeding, schooled in propriety."

"Let me tell you something of my breeding," Kell said with a smile. "My bloodline is about as pure as the cur dog that lives out back of the ranch house. My father was a white trapper who couldn't even write his own name. My mother was a full-blooded Cherokee squaw, driven from her land by a bunch of civilized gentlemen in Washington. High breeding, you say? Not on your life!"

Kell took a sip from his coffee cup. "All this talk of propriety, from an eastern girl, no less. You think we're all barbarians, don't you? Well, let me tell you something, ma'am. Besides the fact you're way too nosy, you've also got a short memory."

"What do you mean?" she asked, bristling at Malone's pointed remarks.

"Where you come from, Miss Payton, so-called gentlemen often settled disputes with guns as well. They called them duels. Sure, the gentlemen always dress better than most of us. Some of them are so darned sophisticated that they lift their little finger when they sip tea. And they rarely butcher the English language, but the results end up being the same. Someone always winds up dead! You call that civilized? But then again, maybe that kind of killing is more to your liking."

Rachel dropped her head. "I suppose I see your point." It galled her to admit that Malone could actually be right.

"Those two men tried to kill me a moment ago, ma'am. But propriety goes out the door when the other man pulls iron. They played the music; I just danced to the tune. Someone had to die and I preferred it to be them. Reckon they got what they deserved!"

"Surely you don't mean that!"

"Yes, ma'am. I mean exactly that! Never once have I drawn on a man first," Kell stated, draining the last of his coffee from the cup. "It's true I've killed a few men in my lifetime. But I never developed a taste for it."

Rachel frowned. "It doesn't seem to bother you much."

"Should it?"

"Yes, I think so. I know you have a heart, Mr. Malone. I saw your gentleness with Lobo."

"Gentleness has nothing to do with what we're talking about. Sure, I'm gentle to a dog, even to my horse. But they never shot at me either.

"You're new to this part of the west, ma'am. Things are different here. Most towns don't even have a sheriff like you've got back east. A man has to stand up for himself. The law's only as good as your ability to defend it.

"When someone straps a gun to his hip, he must also carry the responsibility that goes with it. Those men tried to ambush me and now they're dead. They got what they had coming. You want me to feel some remorse over their death? I'm sorry . . . I just can't."

"I still think you're wrong."

"My only regret is that you still feel that way about it, ma'am."

Kell's arguments had done nothing to sway Rachel's opinion, but it gave her a new perspective from which to look at things. For the first time, Rachel saw Kell's skinned knuckles. "What happened to you?"

"I ran into something."

"I don't suppose it has anything to do with your public bath at the horse trough? Rachel's curiosity was driving her wild.

Malone smiled, but said nothing.

"You're not going to tell me, are you?"

"No, I'm not going to tell you." His eyes twinkled with humor. "Like I told you before . . . you're just too nosy."

Malone's answer further angered the woman. She stormed off towards the kitchen, mad enough to kill someone herself.

Kell smiled to himself, pleased with the result.

***

The rear kitchen door opened under the hand of Clay Adkins. Closely following him was Deke and Julio. Rachel had not been expecting anyone and was startled by their entrance.

"You scared me, Clay."

"I'm sorry," he said.

"Why'd you come in the back door, like someone who had to sneak around?" Seeing the bruises and swelling on Clay's face and knuckles, Rachel forgot all about the question. She then saw the oddly shaped nose. It made her hurt just looking at it. "What happened to you?"

"There was a fight over at the saloon. Just some worthless saddle tramp who spent too long on the bottle. It was nothing."

"It doesn't look like nothing. I think your nose is broken," she replied. Then she noticed the bandage around Deke Hinton's head. "Come on over here and I'll wipe the rest of the blood from your face."

Rachel cleaned away the blood with a damp cloth as Deke and Julio stood next to the door. "You men wait outside for me," Clay ordered. "I'll be right out."

The two men followed his orders without speaking.

"You know what I think of fighting, Clay," Rachel scolded. "And those men . . . why are they always hanging around you? They frighten me. And what happened to that man's head?"

Adkins ignored her. "Has there been anyone here in the diner . . . a stranger, I mean."

"There was earlier, but he just left. It was the man you told me had been killed. Kellen Malone. He said he was looking for his son, Jesse."

Adkins grabbed Rachel, squeezing her arms tightly. His fingers left white marks on her arms. "What did you say?"

"Stop it, Clay! You're hurting me!" she shouted, surprised by her fiancé's sudden burst of rage.

His grip on her arm loosened. "I'm sorry, Rachel."

Rachel remembered the skinned knuckles the stranger had. Then she wondered if Clay had been the one he was fighting.

"I need to talk to you, Clay."

"Well, it will have to wait!" Clay exclaimed coldly. "I have to go now."

"But Malone said . . ."

"I don't care what he says! You shouldn't either!" Going through the door, Adkins muttered halfheartedly, "We'll talk later."

Rachel stood in the middle of the kitchen, bewildered by Clay's sudden, mysterious behavior. "I don't have any idea what's going on," she said to herself, "but I'm certainly going to find out."

***

Once outside the diner and safely out of earshot of Rachel, Adkins spoke to his men. "We've got to hurry. Malone's on his way to the school."

"If he gets in our way," Deke grumbled bitterly, "I'm going to kill him. I owe him for my brother."

"If he gets in our way," Clay added, "I'll help you."

As they mounted their horses, Clay muttered under his breath, "I've got to keep him away from Jesse. I have to!"

Chapter Seven

"How did it go down there?" Stadler asked the young man, who was sitting comfortably in one of the lawyer's fine, leather chairs.

"That depends on who you were rooting for, Malone or the other two. They weren't any match for him with a gun, that's for sure!"

"I wasn't sure he'd live through it."

"I think maybe he's faster now than when he went to prison, Mr. Stadler. And that was with two swollen hands. It'll take more than two men to put him down."

Stadler laughed. "You mean, two of their ilk." The lawyer lifted the brandy he'd been drinking earlier. "Alive or dead, either one served my purposes . . . for the moment anyway. You do have to admit that it makes things interesting to watch."

"You've heard the talk around town, I take it?"

"What talk is that?"

"About Running Hawk. Clements said Malone killed him."

The lawyer rubbed his chin. "That explains everything. If Running Hawk wasn't dead, Malone would be. It's rather a shame about the Indian. He'd been very useful to me."

"If the townsfolk ever find out about your ties to Geronimo and Running Hawk, you're liable to get a bad dose of hemp fever."

"Who's going to tell them?"

Stadler took another drink. "The men Malone shot. Neither one of them got a chance to talk, did they?"

"No, Mr. Stadler. Not that Hinton didn't try."

"Good, very good! And Clay's meeting with Clements? What about that?'

The young man scratched his head. "I couldn't overhear much of the conversation, but I am sure Adkins offered Skull the job."

"No, I don't think so . . . at least, not yet. But what if Skull Clements agrees to work for Adkins and kills Malone? What happens then?"

The lawyer rose from his chair and poured himself another brandy. "May I offer you some?" he asked.

The young man shook his head. "No, thank you. The stuff is good, but I'm just a simple beer drinker myself."

"Suit yourself." Stadler nodded and returned the cap to the expensive liquor decanter. "I came across some interesting information just today," Carlton stated. "It seems that Joe Clements killed three men in Austin, Texas."

"So? He's killed a lot of men everywhere he went."

The lawyer continued. "During the fight, the bartender tried to pull a gun on him. The dead men were named Palance and the bartender was some relation to them. A stranger drew his gun on the bartender, saving Joe's life. That man was none other than our own Kellen Malone."

"Okay," the young man muttered, scratching his head once again. "But what's that got to do with Skull killing Malone?"

"Nothing—not one thing for most gunmen," the lawyer pointed out. "But Clements is not ordinary. Sure the man is highly efficient, stone-cold killer, but he also possesses some other qualities. Some would call them weaknesses. One of those is loyalty to a friend. Joe Clements will not kill Malone, no matter what Adkins offers him."

"You seem mighty sure of yourself."

"I am sure," he said, smugly. "I make it my business to know these things. Always know your enemy, my friend. Any opponent becomes formidable when his traits and character are unknown to you."

"But what if you're wrong about Clements?"

"It wouldn't interfere with my plans. A good poker player just plays the cards he is dealt. His strategies may be altered, but the game remains unchanged. Malone killing Adkins or Adkins killing Malone—either one serves my purposes. Then, we only have to eliminate the survivor."

"What about Clements?"

"He is the wild card in this game." The lawyer laughed crazily. "Him, I may just have to kill myself."

"Skull won't be no pushover; he's killed twenty men."

Stadler tossed down the last of his drink. "I've killed a few also," he replied, smiling like a man recalling a fine memory. "You should be on your way now. So long, Mr. Hodges."

Montana had often questioned the lawyer's sanity, but their conversation had removed any remaining doubts from his mind. Carlton Stadler was insane, but deadly serious with a gun. It made for a lethal combination. In addition, Montana was beginning to wonder about his own mental state, for his involvement in these dealings.

Hodges felt guilty for his betrayal of a friend, but he knew there was no road back. Despite their years of friendship, Montana had no doubts that Malone would kill him if he knew the things he had done. The damage had already been done—a deed which could never be righted. It could only be covered!

***

Joe Clements walked down the street, whistling a tune. He was fresh and clean, following his visit to the bath house. A couple of attractive, young ladies passed him on the board sidewalk and he tipped his hat to each. They smiled at the man, giggling to each other as they continued on their way.

Joe's mind was carefully weighing the offer Adkins had made to him. Still, he hadn't settled on a decision. He decided that his concentration might be clearer after a good night's sleep on a soft, hotel mattress.

As he moved along, Joe saw a man sneaking out of an upstairs office. Clements remembered seeing him earlier in the saloon. Like a man who was ashamed of his actions, the stranger cautiously looked both ways before going down the steps.

Clements, usually a man accustomed to minding his own business, was now curious. Quickly, he slipped back into the shadows to watch.

Joe was sure this was the man he saw earlier. Halstead called him by the name of Montana Hodges. He was sure of it! In fact, Buck also said that Hodges was a close friend of Kellen Malone.

Unaware the man was watching him, Montana came down the steps and continued on his way. Only then did Joe step out of the shadows. Then he headed down the street to the hotel.

Clements rapped on the hotel's counter a couple of times before a sullen, sleepy-eyed clerk shuffled over to his way. The man reminded Clements of a lazy, overfed boar hog.

"May I help you?" the clerk said, sarcastically.

"You sure can," Joe replied. "The name's Clements. I'm supposed to have a room waiting for me."

"Yes, you do. Room three, top of the stairs and to the left. You can't miss it. Sign the register and I'll get your key."

The scent of fried chicken filled the air. Clements saw the clerk's grease-stained shirt. It looks like he's wearing most of it, Joe thought.

"Sorry to interrupt your dinner," Joe said, smiling. He then noticed the chicken leg sticking out of the man's vest pocket.

"It's nothing new. A man can't even eat in peace anymore."

The clerk's greasy fingers handed over the room key. Joe looked disgusted as he took it.

"Just got into town today, huh? I heard you rode in with Kellen Malone. None too choosy about the company you keep, are you, mister?"

Clement's eyes turned cold. He reached across the counter and viciously slapped the man across the mouth.

"Whatever happened between you and Malone is your business and I don't care. But you'd best keep a civil tongue in your head when you talk to me. If you so much as look at me funny again, I'll fry your little hide like that chicken you're eating!"

A lump came to the clerk's throat. He couldn't swallow fast enough to keep it down. In addition, a slow trickle of blood ran from the corner of his lip.

"Now tell me! The upstairs room across the street . . . who lives there?"

"No one lives upstairs," the clerk replied. "A man named Carlton Stadler has a law office there."

Clements wondered what business Montana might have with a lawyer. "Carlton Stadler . . . huh?" Joe turned the name over in his head. He was definitely not familiar with it. "And thanks for your help."

The desk clerk breathed a sigh of relief as the gunman went upstairs. He pulled the drumstick from his pocket, but quickly discovered that he'd lost his appetite.

***

Malone pulled his horse to a stop in front of the tiny, white schoolhouse. On Sundays, church services were held in this same building, as a circuit-riding preacher made his weekly visit to the town of Redhawk. After being gone all these years, Kell wondered if the parson still came to their town. No matter, he thought. His attendance probably wouldn't be any better than it ever was.

Kell walked up the steps quickly, skipping every other one as he went inside. The schoolmarm was busy reading some papers when he entered. She looked to be an elderly woman, with hair as white as winter's first snowfall. Kell guessed she had been witness to about seventy summers.

Seeing her there, Kell removed his hat. He felt nervous and strange, the way he felt as a child whenever he was talking to a teacher.

"Afternoon, ma'am. My name is Kellen Malone."

"Good afternoon to you also," she said cheerfully, while removing her reading spectacles. "Come on in, young man. I already know who you are. You may call me Mrs. Simpson. Mr. Simpson has been gone for many years," she added with a misty eye. "Now it is only me."

The woman was a lonely soul, not unlike himself. She continued talking for several minutes, Kell listening patiently. He also remembered the times he had longed for a sympathetic ear.

"I knew your wife, Alice, quite well, Mr. Malone. We grew to be close friends before her tragic death. She looked after me all the time . . . wouldn't take a penny for it."

Kell nodded, saying nothing.

"She never did believe you were guilty of robbing that stage. Neither do I. A person may learn a lot about someone by the loyalty they inspire in others. You're no thief, Mr. Malone."

Mrs. Simpson paused then, her tired, old eyes staring off into space.

"Please forgive the babblings of a silly, old woman," she said. "I'm so sorry. It's hardly any wonder people hate to talk to me. Sometimes I just go on forever."

"Think nothing of it, Mrs. Simpson. I've enjoyed talking to you. Since coming back to Redhawk, a lot of people haven't seen fit to greet me with open arms."

"You hold your head high, Mr. Malone! You've done nothing wrong. Even if you had, the debt is long since paid." She shook her head. "There I go again. Anyway, what may I do for you, young man?"

"You can start by calling me by my first name. All my friends do."

114

"Okay . . . Kellen."

"I was looking for my son, Jesse, but it's obvious he's already gone."

"Clay Adkins was just here a few minutes before you came. There were a couple of others with him. I think they are not good men," she said, motioning with her hands. "They took your son with them. It appeared to me they were in a hurry."

"Well, thank you for your help, Mrs. Simpson. I'll let you get back to your work."

"Think nothing of it, young man. Yours was a welcomed distraction." As an afterthought, she added, "I live in the small, white frame house next door. I get very few visitors. Therefore, it would be my pleasure to serve you coffee some evening, if it wouldn't trouble you."

Kell smiled, tipping his hat. "You've got a date."

Mrs. Simpson blushed like a schoolgirl. "Come anytime." Her eyes turned serious and the hint of a tear hung in her eye. "Kellen Malone, thank you for taking the time to listen to an old fool."

"Good day to you, ma'am."

As he mounted his horse, Kell mumbled under his breath, "You win this round, Adkins, but the fight is a long way from over.

***

Kell spent the night back on his ranch, camped out next to the mountain spring. As usual, the water flowed freely—clear, fresh, and cold. He deliberately hadn't told anyone where he was going.

He felt safe and peaceful camped out by the spring. With only one accessible entrance, it was difficult to creep up on a man. The way he came could easily be covered by one man with a rifle. The only other means to get there was up the side of a steep mountain. Only a fool would try to scale the mountain from that direction.

With the money Alice had saved for him, he was able to buy some supplies in Redhawk before leaving. For the first time in years, he felt like a wealthy man. He had a side of bacon, flour, sugar, coffee, and several canned goods. Most important of all, he brought along plenty of ammunition. Before this thing was over, Malone had a hunch he would need it.

Taking some of the provisions and ammunition, these he cached in the back of a small cave, which faced the spring. Although it was big enough for two or three people inside, the mouth of the cave was barely big enough for a man to crawl into. Its entrance was obscured by rocks and boulders. So far as he knew, no one had any knowledge of the cave's existence—no one but Jesse.

From this place high on the mountain, he was able to see the lights of his ranch house. He felt a lonely emptiness inside, a desire to return to something that could never be. The ranch was still there, but he felt it would never be the same without his wife and son. Soon he would return. Hopefully, Jesse would have a change of heart and share the place with him. But first, Kell knew he would have to see him and convince him of his innocence. Malone knew it wouldn't be an easy task.

Using his knife for a shovel, he dug a hole in the ground, hoping it would shield and conceal his fire. He filled the hole with sticks and small scraps of paper. In no time at all, he had a fire going.

Earlier, he had snared a couple of jackrabbits. They hung on a spit just above the flames. A pot of coffee was warming there also. Both had just started to smell good.

A few minutes later, he sat down to eat. The coffee was hot, black, and strong, just way he liked it. Although the rabbit was stringy and tough, Kell felt it had prison food beaten all to death. This was the best he could do without firing his gun and drawing unwanted attention to his presence.

As he ate, Kell thought about the day and all that happened. The idea of not seeing Jesse gnawed at his insides. He determined tomorrow would be different! Adkins wasn't about to keep Kell away from his own son. The boy needed to hear the truth; and Kell needed someone to listen. He could only tell his side of the story. It was up to Jesse to decide whether he believed it.

Kell's mind wandered for a little while, filled with thoughts and memories of Alice. They used to come to this place when they were married, the trickling spring being her favorite spot on the ranch. Many a night, Alice and Kell sat in this place together, watching the sun sink over the mountains.

Malone longed to have her with him, to hold her in his arms. Never again, he realized. Alice had gone on ahead, without Kell having the chance to say his goodbyes. Adkins was to blame for his pain and Kell desperately hated him for it!

Another part of him felt solely responsible for her death. If he'd not gone to prison, Kell thought, maybe Alice would still be alive. But what could he have done differently? Would Alice have been better off with her husband on the run, as a wanted man? The questions went on forever. The answers never came.

Kell decided to visit her grave the following day, a chance to finally pay his last respects. It was a chore he dreaded, simply because of the finality of the act. He cursed silently, although there was no one out there to hear his oaths.

After finishing the last of the rabbit, he opened a can of peaches, eating them with his knife. Prison had given him a new appreciation of food—of everything! He thought the King of England never ate anything better than his meal that night.

After dinner, Kell doused his fire, covered the hole he dug, and then went to check on his horse. The animal was right where he picketed him.

His mount had cropped most of the grass around him and his belly appeared full. Malone moved the horse to some fresh grass for the night. Water was close by, in case the animal needed a drink.

Before crawling back into the cave, he took another look down on the ranch house. The lights were out now, Miss Payton having turned in for the night. It was a good idea she had, Kell thought. The day had been a long one.

As Malone pulled the blanket up over his shoulders, his last conscious thoughts were of Jesse . . .

And Rachel.

***

Rachel Payton awoke from her sleep, alive and refreshed, anxious to face a new day. She dressed quickly and combed her hair. She lingered in front of the mirror for a time, as women often do . . . women in love.

When Rachel felt confident she had made the best of her features, she went downstairs, putting a pot of coffee on to heat. The house was a little too cold for her comfort, so she tossed a couple of extra logs on the fire. She stirred the sleeping coals with a poker. They suddenly sprang to life, licking flame onto the new logs she'd added. The logs began to crackle and pop, the cheerful sound bringing instant warmth to her bones.

Twenty minutes later, the smell of ham and eggs filled the sprawling ranch house. As Rachel finished the last of her breakfast, a knock sounded on the door. She recognized the sound of the knock.

"Come on in, Clay. The door's open."

The door opened slowly as Adkins entered the room. Rachel smiled when she saw his face. Her expression soon faded when she noticed the other two men waiting for him outside.

"I thought I smelled coffee, coming up the road." Adkins observed, taking a seat at the table. "Do you have an extra cup handy?"

Rachel noted that he hadn't removed his hat upon entering. She thought it strange. The woman rose from her chair and poured Adkins a cup.

Clay tasted it and smiled. "Thanks, Rachel. Yesterday, you said there was something you wished to discuss with me."

Rachel sat silent for a time, as if something was troubling her. She wanted to believe in her fiancé; she wanted to trust him. Rachel was sure there must be a reasonable explanation for the things she was seeing. She knew Clay would surely put an end to her doubts.

"Mr. Malone was here yesterday."

Adkins froze as if he was in a state of fright. His eyes revealed a hidden rage from deep within his soul, a bitterness that couldn't be hidden. Clay swallowed hard, almost choking on his coffee. "What did he want?" he asked, almost tentatively.

Although Adkins regained his composure quickly, none of these things had escaped Rachel's attention. She wondered about the stranger's return and the change it obviously created in her future husband.

"He told me we had a week to get off his ranch?"

"His ranch?"

"That's what he said, Clay."

"Then we'll see what the sheriff has to say about that."

"Malone said his wife, Alice, hated you and would never sell you the ranch." The question sounded like an accusation.

"And whose word are you going to believe?" Adkins said, his voice flaring in anger. "Are you going to take the word of an outlaw over mine? And why all the questions, Rachel? I feel like I'm on trial here."

"I'm not disputing your word," Rachel explained softly. "Just telling you what the man said. I was also curious as to why you told me Malone had been killed by the Apaches."

"They found a canteen with Malone's name on it in the desert." Adkins hesitated before continuing. "A dead body—a white man's body—was found nearby. That's what made us assume it was him."

Rachel puzzled over the answer. "Yes, Clay, but you told me he was dead a day or so before they brought in the body." She hesitated before speaking. "How could you have possibly known that?"

Clay was angered by her insistence, but he tried to deftly cover his reaction. "I'm sure you are mistaken, dear." He walked towards the window, staring at the horizon, desperately hoping the woman would drop the subject. "It's beautiful out there," Clay observed.

"Yes, it is," she replied. "I love to look out at the mountains."

Clay smiled to himself, pleased that his ploy had worked.

"Before going to bed last night," Rachel continued, "I watched the sunset. It was truly lovely." She walked over to the window, casting her gaze towards the mountains. "There was something strange about it though."

"What do you mean?"

"It looked like there was a light on top of the mountain . . . a campfire or something."

"A campfire . . .?" Clay turned the idea over in his mind.

"Yes, it looked like a flicker of light, but I'm not sure about it. When I looked again later, it was gone," she recounted, still staring off into the distance. "Probably just my imagination or a trick of the night."

She turned away from the window. "How does your face feel today, Clay? It looks terribly painful."

Adkins said nothing, his mind still pondering the possibilities about the campfire. After a few seconds, he asked, "What was that you said?"

"Your face . . . how does it feel?"

"It's a little sore, but I'll live."

"Yesterday, on my way to the diner, I saw Mr. Malone washing himself at the horse trough. He looked like he'd been in a fight. Do you know anything about it?" Rachel asked, after already hearing some gossip about their fight.

"Yes," answered Clay. "Kellen Malone is the barbarian who attacked me in the saloon. Without provocation, I might add! Yet it just didn't seem important enough to worry you about."

Increasingly, the woman's questions were growing more pointed and accusative. Clay softly cursed the name of Kellen Malone. He longed for the conversation to be over.

"I don't understand you, Clay. We're about to be married and you act as though you're hiding things from me."

"I'm not hiding anything from you!" he blurted out.

Adkins suddenly raised his hand, as if to strike her. A knock on the door stopped him. It was Julio.

Rachel felt relieved for the sudden interruption.

"Jesse's out here, Boss," Julio announced.

"Send him on in," Adkins declared. In a whispered tone, he added, "Don't you ever interfere in my business again, Rachel. Do you understand?"

Jesse came in the door quickly with Lobo following behind. "You sent for me, Mr. Adkins?"

For the first time, Rachel noticed how closely the boy mirrored his father's features. His hair was dark, eyes brown, just like Malone. Another similarity was the boy's jawbone; strong, firm, and clearly defined. He was obviously growing to be a fine, young man.

"I want you to stay here today, Jesse," Adkins said. "Hang around the ranch, son. School will get along fine without you for a day."

"Do you really mean it, sir?"

"Yes, I do, Jesse. Enjoy your day."

Rachel wanted to protest his decision, but after Clay's latest outburst, she grudgingly decided against it.

"I will, sir." The boy hesitated for a moment before inquiring, "Mr. Adkins, do I have to talk to my pa?"

"Not if you don't want to, son." Clay did his best to look concerned for the boy's welfare and played the role to perfection. "I intend to make sure he stays away from all of us."

"Thank you, Mr. Adkins."

"I'm glad to do this for you, Jesse. Maybe you can go riding later. Feel free to take any of the horses in the stable."

The boy nodded, obviously pleased with the idea of missing school for a day. He went towards the door, followed by Lobo. The dog growled softly as he passed by Adkins.

Suddenly, Rachel could constrain herself no longer. "Any father has a right to see his son. Even Mr. Malone."

"No!" he said bitterly. "I won't allow it. I took Jesse out of school yesterday, just to keep Malone away from him. The man is nothing but trouble."

"But you have no right . . ."

"I have every right!" Clay said, cutting her off in mid-sentence. "I am merely looking out for the boy's interests. There will be no more discussion of it."

Rachel watched as Adkins headed towards the door. She had never seen this side of the man's nature before; the cruelty, mystery, and deceit. Even the dog didn't like him. Rachel suddenly saw her fiancé with new eyes.

That he had lied to her, she had no doubt. Clay's dishonesty cast a whole new light on everything he ever told her. She was beginning to have some serious misgivings about Clay, not that they hadn't always been there, lurking just beneath the surface. It took the stranger's arrival to bring these traits into the open.

She remembered what Malone had said the first day they met, about not harnessing herself to a liar. It was sound advice. Whatever else the man might be, Malone had been true to his word. Rachel could no longer say the same thing about Clay Adkins.

***

Malone was awakened by a muffled, rustling noise prowling around his campfire. Instantly, his hands went to his six-guns. The noise grew louder, closer, nearing the mouth of the cave.

Kell quietly moved that way to investigate. Easing his way to the cave's entrance, he could see the first, bright rays of sunlight making their way inside. Still, he could see nothing of the mysterious intruder.

If the man's intentions were friendly, Kell was sure he wouldn't come skulking into camp like a common thief. Aside from the fact it revealed a serious lack of character, it also gave the intruder a better than average chance of meeting his maker.

Malone holstered one of his guns. Taking great care to keep his barrel out of the dirt, he crawled on all fours towards the cave's only entrance. Immediately upon leaving the safety of the cave, he would be exposed and vulnerable, a likely target for a bullet. No matter, Kell thought. His horse was out there and he hated to walk.

Whispering a few quick words to the guardian of fools, Kell made his move. He dived out of the cave, gun cocked and ready . . .

A mountain lion was prowling around outside the cave, looking for her morning's breakfast. Although the man-smell must have bothered her, the lion had been so committed to her hunt, she had ignored the bothersome scent.

When she saw Malone, the cat jumped a couple of feet into the air. The lion made tracks for parts unknown, its hunger all but forgotten.

He lay there on the ground in his longjohns, six-gun drawn, the gun-belt slung around his hips. He wore nothing but a battered hat, dirty socks, and a stupid expression.

"Must have been the most awful sight that critter ever saw," Kell muttered. "That old she-cat is jumpier than I am." Malone laughed until his sides hurt.

***

Clay was glad to finally be out of the house. Rachel was starting to ask too many questions and the explanations were growing more difficult. He started for his horse, with Deke and Julio matching him step for step. A fire on the mountain, he thought. Things were finally starting to go his way. A confident smile sprang to his face.

"Deke, you and Julio are going to be busy tonight," Adkins said smugly. "I think I know where to find Kellen Malone."

Chapter Eight

Joe Clements was an early riser, arriving at the diner the following morning before it opened for business. As was his habit anywhere, he chose a table in the back. The location gave him the first view of anyone entering the place.

A creature of habit, Clements grew accustomed to routine, the way one might grow comfortable with an old hat or a run-down pair of boots. He also realized that predictability could be a deadly trait for the hunted. Habits can be studied and routine exploited. Unable to change his nature and unwilling to die, Joe's only habits became ones of caution and unpredictability.

Joe seldom left a room the same way he entered. He never followed the same trail twice in a row and he always lived for the moment. He continually planned for tomorrow; he never expected to see it.

When the food was brought to him, Joe ate like starved wolves tearing at a carcass during a blizzard. As he sopped up the last of the gravy with a buttermilk biscuit, Clay Adkins entered the room. Deke and Julio followed him.

Joe looked up from his plate, nodding at Clay, but deliberately ignoring the other two. He smiled to himself as he saw their expressions, knowing it rankled them some.

Clements felt no love for Clay Adkins but he had to give the man some credit. Clay was a builder, a man who started towns and created empires. Although these were often established at the expense and suffering of smaller, less prosperous men, that knowledge did nothing to diminish the man's accomplishments in Joe's eyes.

Deke and Julio were a different story altogether. Joe had known many men of their sort—parasites—ones who lived off the work of others. He had also buried many like them, never with any remorse. His feelings for them ran to nothing but contempt.

"What brings you out so early, Clay?"

"You do, Joe."

"Then pull up a seat," Joe said, taking a sip of coffee. "Maybe order some breakfast."

Adkins pulled back a chair. Deke and Julio did likewise.

The look in Clements' eyes froze them where they stood. "I didn't say anything about you two sitting down," he said coldly. "You boys just wait outside."

"Now wait just a minute, Skull!" Adkins flared. "Hinton and the breed work for me. They go where I tell them."

"Then tell them to go away! I don't care who they work for, Clay. But I am a mite choosy about those I eat with." Clements didn't waver. The men didn't move. "You'd better send them to a place they want to go, before I send them to a place they don't."

"Go on . . . wait for me up front," Clay relented. "Get yourself a cup of coffee and tell them it's on me. I'll be along in a few minutes."

Grudgingly, the two of them did as they were told. A pair of proud men, both still wanted to push the issue.

"You're taking a big chance, Skull. Those two are crazy, especially the breed. You kicked them out of the way like they were a couple of stray dogs."

"What if I did?"

"Dogs are known to bite back."

"I shot the last dog that bit me."

"You know why I'm here." Impatiently, Adkins began to tap his fingers on the table. "You've had all night, Skull. What will it be?"

Clements downed the last bite of biscuit and drank his coffee. Then he stared off into space as if he hadn't heard. Finally, he stared Adkins directly in the eye.

"Your offer was a fair one, Clay. But the answer is no."

"What do you mean . . . no?" You've already been paid. I gave you five thousand dollars for Malone's hide!" Adkins fought down the anger that was building inside him. "It will be easy, Skull. You can even take Deke and Julio with you. I don't care about the details, just so he's dead."

"Let me tell you something, Clay. Malone will never be easy to take, no matter what you do." He quickly broke into a smile. "And if I have to take those two limp saddlehorns with me, it'll cost you about fifty thousand for the job."

"Look, Skull, I don't have much time for dickering. Rachel will be here to start work soon. I'll give you two thousand more when the job is done."

Clements just shook his head. "It's tempting, but the answer's still the same."

Adkins jumped to his feet, his face twisted in rage. "A couple of my men will be over later to pick up the money."

"Don't bother."

"What do you mean by that?"

"Coming here cost me another job, Clay. I have expenses to cover. And about that money underneath the floorboards . . . how can I be sure it belongs to you?" Clements smiled at the man facing him. "Some poor, unfortunate soul might have hidden it there, planning to get it later. I turned it over to the sheriff for safekeeping. Said I could pick it up later, providing no one lays claim to it."

Clements had been rolling a smoke as he talked. He stuck it between his lips, striking a match on the leg of his chair. As he lit the cigarette, he smiled over his cupped hand. There was a look of challenge on his face. "You and I both know there ain't nobody gonna claim that money, don't we?" Joe shrugged his shoulders. "Those are the risks you take whenever you start dealing with shady characters like me.

"But let no man say that Joe Clements ain't an honest man. You just call the money a down payment, Clay. Depending on the work, the next couple of jobs will come free. Fair enough?"

"You won't get away with this, Skull. I'll see you dead!"

"It appears that I've already gotten away with it. And about that matter of seeing me dead . . . my money's on you dying first." Clements took a couple of deep pulls on his cigarette. "It's been a pleasure doing business with you."

"This isn't over!" Adkins blurted out, as he stormed out of the diner. In his hurry to leave, Clay didn't notice the dark figure standing in the shadows outside.

***

Kell saddled his horse and started down the road to Redhawk. There were a lot of things he needed to do today and he wanted to get an early start.

More and more, Malone found himself thinking about the woman living at the ranch. Kell knew he was kidding himself, thinking a woman like that would ever care for him. And besides, he told himself, Rachel would be married soon—married to Clay Adkins. But it made no difference to him, he reasoned. He cursed softly at the thought.

Daydreaming was a luxury he couldn't afford, not for a man living in wild country. It was also a bad idea for a man surrounded by this many enemies. Reaching down towards his thigh, he slipped the rawhide thongs off the hammers of his six-guns. It never hurt to be too careful.

Twice, Clay Adkins and his men had tried to kill him. He rode along carefully, stopping every few minutes to check his backtrail. Clay had failed yesterday, but those failures wouldn't prevent him from trying again. Failed again . . . he turned the thought over in his mind.

For the first time, Kell began to question Clay's motive for wanting him dead. It was true that they hated each other, but it had to be more than that. Most obvious of all, Adkins wanted to own the ranch. But was that all? Then it hit him . . .

Adkins was threatened by his presence; by what he might know and what he might discover. Maybe he would find out who really robbed the stage and why they did it. Kell kicked himself for never thinking of it before.

Slapping the spurs to his mount, Malone galloped down the trail towards Redhawk. A shot sounded behind him. Kell had no idea if the bullet had been meant for him. But he had no intention of waiting for another. He reined his horse into a low spot in the trail. The horse's tail stretched out long behind him in the wind. Kell had a man to see . . .

Sheriff Bill Kimball.

A couple of minutes later, Malone jerked back on the reins in front of the sheriff's office. The animal stopped so quickly the hooves kicked up dust. Out of the saddle before the mustang came to a complete stop, Kell charged into the sheriff's office.

The sheriff looked up with a start. "Back when I was a youngster," Kimball said dryly, "we used to knock on a door before we tore it off the hinges. But then again, young folks had manners back in those days."

"Sorry about that, Bill." The look on his face was one of shame. "Reckon I had something on my mind."

"Hate to think you ruined a good door for nothing," he said with a smile. "It's really no problem, Kell. I wanted to see you anyway." Kimball walked over to the stove and poured himself a cup of coffee. Steam rose from the tin cup as he poured. "You want some?"

Malone nodded and reached out to take it.

"Why did you want to see me, Bill?" he asked, taking a sip of the hot coffee. It nearly burned the hide off his tongue.

Without speaking, Kimball reached into his desk. Removing an object from inside the drawer, this he placed on the desk. "This belongs to you."

Malone recognized it immediately. It was his gold watch.

"I've had that ever since the trial," Bill explained. "It was the one piece of evidence used to convict you. It keeps good time, but it cost you seven years of your life."

"That and Clay Adkin's testimony," Kell added. "Him claiming to recognize my voice." He stared at the watch for second, then shoved it into his vest pocket.

"How do you suppose it got there, Kell? I know you didn't rob the stage."

"Here, lately, I've been giving that a lot of thought. I haven't been able to come up with a single answer . . . just more questions. But that brings me to what I wanted to talk to you about."

Kimball rose from his chair once again. "Here, let me warm that up for you again," the sheriff said, grabbing the cup from Kellen's hand. He poured more coffee into the tin cup, before handing it back to Malone. "Now go ahead and speak your mind, Kell."

As if it wasn't hot enough already, Kell thought. He looked at the cup with a scowl. The glance was then directed at Kimball. "Man! That stuff is hotter than the shaded side of Hades," Kell muttered, before continuing. "My father never had much of what the world calls education. And he died while I was still mighty young. Still, he taught me some things. One of them is how to read a trail. But I can't seem to follow this one. There's a whole herd of things about this robbery that just don't tally up right."

"What do you mean?"

"The stage wasn't carrying any strongbox and the passengers said they lost nothing of any real value. They didn't even take the young girl's jewelry." Malone scratched his head. "Let me ask you something, Bill. Would you risk going to prison, a hangman's rope, or a stomach full of buckshot just to steal a few dollars?"

He laughed. "It'd surely be a mite stupid, wouldn't it?"

"It sure would." Malone swallowed the last of Kimball's wicked brew. "I want you to tell me everything you can remember about the trial."

"There ain't too much to tell you that you don't already know."

"That's fine. Just go over it again, in case I've forgotten anything. When a man starts digging, he always tosses away whatever's on the surface. Maybe misses the obvious."

The sheriff kicked his feet up on the desk and leaned back in his chair. Then he began. "The stage was headed east to Redhawk, carrying five passengers. Clay Adkins was one of them. One of them was a salesman, I think. There were also two women and a young girl, going to see her relatives.

"The stage was making good time that day, the driver said. They were ten minutes ahead of schedule . . . kind of unusual for that grumpy, old man. Anyway, just as they crossed Ocotillo Pass, three masked riders swarmed down in their path."

Kimball built a smoke and resumed his story. "The shotgun guard wanted to throw down on the outlaws, but Haisley wouldn't let him take the risk. Since they were carrying no strongbox, old man Haisley saw no reason to make a fight of it. Haisley's a smart one—you have to give him that. The boy was young and eager, spoiling for a fight, like a lot of kids we've seen planted."

"Anything else you can think of?"

"Well, they said the ringleader was a tall, lean rascal, just like you. He did most of the talking. That's how I knew it wasn't you . . . he talked too much.

"Anyway, one of the bandits walked with a limp. The other guy was short and stocky. The three of them relieved the women of their valuables and whatever money the passengers were carrying. Then they rode away, but not before one of them called the boss by name . . . the name of Kell."

"Tell me about the man who had the limp."

"There's really nothing to tell. When the bandits got off their horses, the shotgun guard noticed one of them had a bum leg."

"Like Sam Hinton, you mean?"

"Hey! I think you're on to something. If I read the trail right, then you're figuring Deke was the other one. He's short and stocky, just like the witnesses said."

"I'd lay money on it."

"Shame nobody cared about the truth seven years ago. Everyone was anxious to pin the robbery on someone and they were too quick to believe Clay Adkins. And you . . . a half-breed Indian." Kimball shook his head in disgust. "They didn't need anything else. Just wish things could have been different."

"I don't blame you at all, Bill."

"You don't know how much I appreciate hearing you say that, Kell. I was just a young deputy then, barely dry behind the ears. The whole thing didn't read right to me, but the sheriff insisted you were guilty. When I argued the subject, he found some lousy excuse to send me away until the trial was over."

"Yeahhhhhh, I know it," Kell mumbled. "There's still a couple of pieces missing, Bill. Who was the outlaw who passed himself off as me? Why did they do it? And how did my watch get there?"

"We may never find the answer to those questions," Kimball said with a shrug. "Even if we did, knowing them and proving them would be two different things."

"Well, someone's getting a mite antsy. They tried to bushwhack me yesterday and someone took a shot at me a while ago."

"A shot?"

"Yeah, Bill. It happened on my way to town."

"You get a look at 'em?"

"No, I didn't. I was too busy getting out of there."

"You think it was Skull Clements?"

"Joe Clements never shied away from killing anyone, but he's no back shooter. I can tell you that for sure, Bill."

"Clay was here to see me yesterday, Kell."

"He was? I always thought he fought shy of lawmen he didn't own."

Kimball, normally in good humor, didn't smile this time. "Adkins wanted to file a complaint. He says you're threatening him, telling him and Miss Rachel to get off the ranch. Is that true, Kell?"

"It's my ranch, Bill. Alice would never sell it, especially not to a dirty, stinking polecat like Adkins."

"Clay has a deed to the ranch, clear and legal. I've seen it myself."

"I don't care if it's written on stone tablets!" Kell snapped back. "It ain't worth the paper it's scribbled on, Bill. Something about this whole thing stinks."

"What happened to all the money Alice received for the ranch? There were a lot of beeves, too. What about them? Alice should have been wealthy woman. Instead, she found herself taking in sewing and odd chores."

Kimball walked to the window and stared outside. "The papers were drawn up by Carlton Stadler, according to law. They were even witnessed by the Hinton brothers. I don't like it either, Kell, but they look genuine to me. Until I can prove otherwise, the ranch belongs to Adkins."

Malone jumped from his seat, mad enough to kill. "Don't you see, Bill? Adkins fine hand is all over this. Both of these boys work for Clay. Sam Hinton tried to kill me yesterday, probably with Clay's blessing—and at his urging. Now you're telling me that Alice sold Clay the ranch. No! I won't accept it!"

"I'm warning you, Kell," said Kimball, his face turning red with anger. "Don't you push the issue . . . or our friendship. If you continue to bother Adkins, I'll have to arrest you. Don't make me do that!"

"You do what you have to, Bill. So will I." His face was determined. "I've been on the wrong side of the law before. I'm beginning to get used to it."

Neither of them said anything for a minute, a pair of hardheads, unwilling to budge or compromise. Each of them knew the other would do what he felt necessary, no matter what the consequences might be.

"Not to change the subject or anything, Kell, but I've got to tell you something that happened. Skull Clements came in to see me this morning. He claimed someone left five thousand dollars under the floorboards of his hotel room. He asked me to keep it for him, unless someone reported it missing."

"The man's just a model citizen, isn't he?" Malone chuckled out loud. "Makes a body wonder how he came to look under the floorboards anyway."

"That's the same thing I was thinking, Kell. It set me to wondering. What do you suppose it costs to hire a gunman like Clements?"

"Probably a couple of thousand dollars, depending on the job and who he has to kill. Reckon the price might go higher, if the murder has to be done real fast."

"Sure pays better than keeping the peace," said Kimball.

"There are a lot of things happening in Redhawk right now," Kell muttered. "Most of them don't make much sense. But they all have one thing in common . . . and that's Clay Adkins. You think about that." Malone rose from his seat and headed for the door. "Thanks for the coffee."

"Kell, about the deed . . ." The remark froze Malone in the door. "I'd almost forgotten. Besides the Hinton brothers, there was another name as witness on that deed. It's the one reason I never questioned whether the paper was authentic. With him as a witness, I figured it had to be for real."

"Who was it, Bill?"

"Montana Hodges."

Malone was speechless as he left the sheriff's office.

***

Having just finished the last of his morning's coffee, Joe Clements rose from his seat. As he placed the money for his meal on the table, a well-dressed man approached the table. Joe appraised the stranger carefully, taking note of the man's fine appearance. Normally, Clements would have taken him for a gentleman. The well-worn, walnut handled revolver, peeking from underneath his coat tails said otherwise.

Clements knew the breed of man he was facing. He recognized something in the stranger's face and mannerisms . . . a sense of awareness and caution. They were qualities he also possessed. The man's clothes, freshly cleaned and pressed, did nothing to conceal the wolfish individual who lurked beneath their disguise. Clements knew . . .

The stranger was a gunman.

"And you would be Joe Clements?"

"Yes, I am," Clements answered, once again sitting back down in his chair.

"If you'll excuse me, my name is Carlton Stadler. I am an attorney here in Redhawk."

"So?"

"Do you mind if I sit down?"

"Suit yourself."

"I understand you had some past business dealings with Clay Adkins, Mr. Clements. I was standing outside a moment ago and I saw him leave."

"Yeah, that's right," Joe replied coldly. "But my business is just that . . . it's my business!"

"You misunderstand me, sir. It is not my wish to pry in your affairs. I am private in my dealings also. I seek only to hire you, if you are not already so employed."

"You've got my attention. Keep talking."

By this time, Rachel had arrived at the diner. After tying on her apron, she made her way over to their table. "May I help you, gentlemen?"

"Nothing for me, thank you," Stadler replied.

"Same goes for me, ma'am."

Carlton watched Rachel as she walked away, his eyes leering at her figure wickedly. "Shame that woman wants to marry Adkins," the lawyer observed. "I'd like to waltz her around a little myself."

"Leave the woman alone," Joe warned sternly, his green eyes turning hard. "Talk that way around me again and I'll kill you."

Stadler just smiled, his expression showing no concern over Joe's threat. "You can't talk that way to me. I am an officer of the court."

"No, you're not, Stadler. You're just another smooth-talking shyster."

Something in the lawyer's eyes gave away his reaction. Clements knew he had touched a nerve.

"You don't approve of me, I take it?"

"No, Stadler. I don't approve of your profession."

"And why might that be?"

"The world used to be a simple place. Now we have you lawyers crawling out the woodwork like roaches. No one speaks for himself any more. A man's word and handshake means nothing, thanks to men like you, Stadler.

"Settle your differences in a courtroom, they say. Disputes used to be settled like gentlemen, with fists or a gun. Questions of honor were cleared right up, face to face. The results were a whole lot more permanent and not nearly as dirty."

"You're entitled to your opinion, Mr. Clements. Perhaps we shall have occasion to discuss this matter further." A veiled threat lay hidden beneath the false-front of Stadler's smile. "My work forces me to have dealings with all manner of individuals. Some of these men are, shall we say, less than savory. Occasionally, I could use a man of your skills."

"You're taking the long way home, mister! I'm sure there's a point to this conversation somewhere. Some folks might think you're a real, smooth talker, but I'm not buying any. I think you're just about as subtle as a corncob in an outhouse.

"I'm a gunman, Mr. Stadler . . . a hired killer. Nobody ever hired me for my good works and charming personality. I ain't no good at small talk and I make doggone bad company! And I like it that way." Clements looked around the room, to make sure that nobody was close enough to hear them. "So why don't we cut this Honest Abe act and get right down to the point of this here conversation. Now, who do you want killed?"

"Okay," Stadler said. "I'll be blunt. I'll give you five thousand dollars to kill Kellen Malone. You can have a couple thousand now and rest when the job is done."

Clements scratched his head. For a man who'd been gone for seven years, Malone sure had a lot of enemies. Joe was beginning to think everyone in town wanted Kell dead.

"If I go after Malone, it will cost you ten thousand bucks. I can tell you that right now, Stadler."

"Ten thousand dollars? That's extortion."

"No, Mr. Stadler. That's business. If it's too rich for you, I'll understand."

"Okay! Okay! Ten thousand it is."

Joe did his best to keep a straight face. "Tell me something, Stadler. Why me? You and I both know you're a gunman. I've run all the names through my head, all the good ones. Stadler isn't one of them, but it'll come to me. You could kill him yourself. Better yet, let Hodges do it. That would be better . . . Malone trusts him."

"I don't know what you're talking about, Mr. Clements."

"Yeah, you do, Stadler. I saw him come sneaking out of your office yesterday. It got me to wondering . . ."

"Well, like you said, Joe. My business is just that . . . it's my business."

Joe ignored Stadler's comment. "It got me to wondering what a friend of Malone's would be doing talking to you. After asking around, I found out that you're the lawyer who defended Malone. Sent him straight to prison, you did. Now, if I was Malone, I wouldn't want any of my friends getting cozy with you."

Stadler, who prided himself on remaining cool under pressure, was starting to get a little irritated. Clements was calmly enjoying the show.

"Listen, Joe! Do you want the job or not?"

"I ain't made up my mind yet. You'll have to tell me what you want done first."

"Clay Adkins has become something of a liability to me," Stadler explained. "Later this afternoon, Clay is going to be killed."

"Why all this sudden desire to kill Adkins?" Joe interrupted. "From what I've seen, Malone may just do it for nothing."

When Malone came back to Redhawk, that is exactly what I hoped would happen. But Malone has some scruples about him and won't kill a man in cold blood. From what I've heard, those same attributes don't apply to you, Mr. Clements."

Stadler watched the scar-faced gunman to see what kind of reaction his remark would produce. Clements never even blinked.

"Adkins is going to be killed. We may shoot him in the back, like he was murdered from ambush. One of my men will handle that. But it really doesn't matter how he gets it." Stadler smiled, obviously pleased with himself. "Malone will undoubtedly get the blame for Clay's murder. Everybody knows he hated Adkins. And that is where you come in."

"When the sheriff deputizes a posse, you see that you're on it. From there, all you have to do is make sure Malone doesn't get a trial. You can say he was shot trying to escape. No one will dare say any different, for fear of calling you a liar."

"Ain't that tidy! You've thought of everything now, haven't you, Stadler?"

"Loose ends always have a way of unraveling. I don't like that, Mr. Clements. Now will you take the job?"

"Bring the money to my hotel room later," Clements muttered.

"You remember those loose ends I was talking about, Mr. Clements? I suggest you don't become one."

Clements laughed out loud at the lawyer's threat. Then his attention was suddenly drawn out the window, watching the tall figure approaching the diner.

Chapter Nine

As Malone walked into the diner, he immediately noticed the two men in the back. It struck him as strange, two such men sharing a table, different as their professions were. Then another thought came to him. Maybe the two men weren't so different after all, just a couple of hired guns.

Both of their vocations represented some kind of law. Either one of them could be purchased if the money was right. One of the men made a living pleading for justice. The other merely dispensed it.

"Why, there's the noble barrister himself." Malone bellowed out sarcastically. "Now what kind of business would an honest lawyer possibly have with a hired gun?" He smiled at Clements. "No offense, Joe."

Clements chuckled at Kell's remark. "None taken."

Curious as to the sudden disturbance, Rachel and the cook stared from the doorway. Malone's voice lowered not one bit.

"Good morning, Mr. Stadler," Kell said. "Win any big cases lately? Draw up any more deeds for Clay Adkins? You cheat any more helpless women, while their husbands rotted away in prison?"

Malone knew Stadler had given him a poor defense in court. So along with Adkins, Kell blamed the lawyer for his wife's death. Still nursing a grudge, Malone was pushing Stadler hard, hoping to prompt a fight. He wanted the lawyer to fight, to strike back—anything to give him an excuse. Most of all, Kell hoped he would go for a gun.

His face twisted in anger, Stadler rose from his chair. The lawyer's hand hung at his right side, inches away from the bulge underneath his coattail. Malone could see that his remarks were beginning to have their desired effect.

Despite his pride, Stadler finally gained his composure. "You shouldn't go around making unsubstantiated allegations like that, Mr. Malone. There's not a shred of evidence to back your charges.

"By the way, slander is against the law. It can also be a very dangerous thing . . . from a legal standpoint, I mean." The tone of his voice, although quiet and reserved, unmistakably contained a warning. "A man of your reputation, Mr. Malone, doesn't need any more trouble with the law . . . or with me."

Like any predator, Stadler always grew quiet before an attack. The low tone of his voice and the fire in his eyes was enough to ward off most men. Kell was simply too stubborn to heed the signs. The harder an animal tried to buck him off, the more Malone dug in his spurs.

"I know all about the law, Stadler. I've just had seven long years of lessons." Kell walked right up to him, staring the man down the way two mountain bucks might eye each other during the breeding season. "The law, you say. I've had more than a bellyful of it crammed down my throat, mister, dished out and spoon fed by the likes of you!"

The lawyer desperately wanted to push the issue; Malone could see it. But witnesses were present and the lawyer preferred to employ his strategies in private. Although he found it distasteful, Stadler fought down his instincts. There would be another time to deal with Kellen Malone. He had only to wait.

As Stadler put on his hat, Malone noticed he did everything with his left hand, always keeping his gunhand free. It was a common trait for men of the gun. Malone generally practiced it himself.

The lawyer threw a bitter scowl at Kell. He then walked around him, glancing over his shoulder. "This is your lucky day, Malone," Stadler said, smiling. "Enjoy it while you still can."

Silently, Malone and Clements watched him walk out the door of the diner.

"Put you to mind of a rattler, doesn't he?" Joe remarked. "Calm one minute, then sinking a fang in you the next."

"The man may be a lawyer now," Kell observed thoughtfully, "but he's sniffed more than his share of gunsmoke. Man doesn't get a calloused thumb that way, not unless he's eared back a few hammers on a shootin' iron." He pulled back a chair and sat down.

"Yeah, Malone. You've got a good eye. That's the way I read it too. I know Stadler's a shootist, but I can't seem to pin a name on him."

"If you come up with anything, I'd count it as personal favor if you'd fill me in, Joe. It'd be a plus to know who you're going up against."

"Sure thing, Malone." Clements hesitated before speaking, searching for a better way to say what was on his mind. Coming up empty, he just blurted it out. "How did you know that Adkins was going to hire me to kill you?"

"I didn't know for sure. Until now, that is," Malone said, grinning. "I had a hunch. That's all." Kell wanted to ask if he'd taken the job, but he wouldn't. "I meant what I said, Joe. I wouldn't want to kill you."

Clements seemingly read his mind. "Just in case you want to know, I turned Clay down, Malone. Not that I'm afraid of you or anything, but Joe Clements always pays his debts. You can breathe easy now; I won't be gunning for you." The scar-faced gunman broke into a smile. "You saved my life before. Reckon that makes us even."

"You're taking a lot for granted, Joe," Kell said with a smile. "I'm not so sure you could take me."

Clements laughed. "Me, neither. Would make for a heckuva show, you've got to admit." The gunman eyed him strangely. "Tell me something, Kell. Why didn't you just shoot me back on the trail? No one would ever have known. We both know you had plenty of chances."

"Never did kill anyone in cold blood, Joe. Guess I'm not ready to start now."

"But how did you know I wouldn't take Clay's money and then come gunning for you?"

"I didn't know. Had to find out for myself. Guess you could say I took a chance on you, Joe. It must have been a darned good wager."

"Well, I don't know if I could have done the same, Malone. You ain't gonna catch me riding with someone out to kill me," Joe got up to leave, then stopped, like a man with something else on his mind. "It's none of my business," he asked, "but how well do you know Hodges?"

"Montana? Him and me, we go back a number of years together," Kell explained. "Next to Buck Halstead, Montana's the nearest thing I've got to a brother. Why're you asking?"

"No reason, really," replied Joe, scratching his head. "It's just that people change sometimes and not always for the better. A man thinks he knows someone and then time passes. Next thing you know, the person changes. Same face, different person. No real reason for it, I guess. It just happens.

"Well, you be sure and watch your step, Malone," Joe said. "Lot of folks in this town would like to see you dead. And don't forget one thing . . ."

"What's that?" asked Malone.

"Cain killed *his* brother."

***

When Carlton Stadler returned to his office, he found Montana Hodges waiting for him there. The young cowhand was sitting in the lawyer's fine chair, his feet propped up on the desk.

"Believe in making yourself at home, don't you?"

The young man grinned. "How did it go with Skull?"

"He agreed to kill Malone, just like I thought he would," related Stadler, shoving Montana's feet off the desk. "And get out of my chair!"

Montana moved to one of the other chairs, one nearly as plush as the one he vacated. "But I thought you told me Skull wouldn't kill Malone."

"You still don't understand, do you?" Stadler said. The young man curiously studied the lawyer's face. "It just proves Clements can't be trusted . . . not by us anyway. The man was just pumping me for information."

"Information? For what reason?"

"My guess would be that he feels some obligation or loyalty to Adkins, after working so much for him in the past. Although he wouldn't accept Clay's offer to kill Malone, Clements might think he should warn Clay of my intentions."

Hodges shook his head. "From what I know of the man, Skull comes with the reputation of being tight-lipped. I don't believe he'll say anything."

"That may well be so, but we cannot take any chances. Tell your associates that Malone must die tonight. I wanted a posse to kill him, so there would be no possible link to me," explained Stadler. "But this will work just as well and Malone will be just as dead."

"Deke and Julio know where he's staying at night, but I want you to make sure everything goes according to plan. First, you get rid of Adkins. What he knows might bury both of us."

"And what about Skull, Mr. Stadler?"

The lawyer laughed deeply. "If Clements gets in the way, then I'll kill him. "I'm surprised he doesn't remember me. We ran into each other once, back east. Yes, sir," he said with a chuckle. "I figure killing him will be a real pleasure.

"And speaking of pleasure . . . then there's that Payton woman. Shame for her to be left alone like that. Someone's going to have to take care of her after Clay's dead."

The usually jovial eyes of the young cowhand took on an unusual seriousness. "You'd better forget the woman, Stadler," Montana offered. "It'll lead to nothing but trouble."

"That sounds funny coming from you," roared the lawyer. "Malone's woman is the thing that got you into this mess. You do know he'll kill you, don't you . . . if he ever finds out, I mean?"

"Yeah, I know," he mumbled. "Can't say I'd blame him much. I just want to get this thing over with and out of the way. With Kell dead, maybe I'll be able to forget what happened."

"If you follow my instructions, this whole thing will be over by to-morrow."

"I surely hope so."

Stadler sipped his drink. "I still find it hard to believe you don't have a weakness for the Payton woman, with her looking so much like Alice Malone."

"I never meant to kill her. Yeah, I wanted her; I'll admit that. But her death changed everything. It changed me." Montana wrung his hands together nervously. "Probably never feel the same way about a woman again. Wish I could turn back the clock."

"You think he suspects you?"

"No, I don't think so, Mr. Stadler. Kell and I have been friends for a long time. He'd have no reason to suspect me of anything." Hodges paused at the door before leaving. "I'll let you buy me a drink tonight, after I kill . . . when it's all over. I figure I'll be needing one.

"Meant what I said about the woman, Mr. Stadler." Increasingly, Montana was troubled by the pangs of conscience. He hoped his pleas in Rachel's behalf would somehow make amends for Alice Malone's death. Hodges knew he had gone too far—fallen in too deep to ever claw his way back. It was all he knew to do. "Please don't harm Miss Payton."

"You have my word, Mr. Hodges. No harm will come to her," he said.

Montana nodded. "Thank you," he said, before walking out the door.

Stadler tossed down the last of his drink. "No, Mr. Hodges, I won't harm one hair on her pretty little head . . . not until I'm satisfied, anyway."

A hideously insane laugh could be heard coming from the lawyer's office.

***

After Joe Clements left the diner, Malone was troubled by his questions about Hodges. Mostly, Malone was troubled by the things Joe deliberately *didn't* say. Kell knew there had been a none-too-subtle message lurking behind the question. Maybe it was a just a hunch. Perhaps it was a warning. He felt sure that Joe had tried to warn him of something—or someone . . .

Of Montana.

Joe Clements hadn't lived this long by chance. Like Malone, he was a gunfighter. Cool and collected during any kind of a fight, the only thing about him to go off half-cocked might be his gun. Good instincts were essential to a gunman's survival, possibly more necessary than his skill and speed with a gun. Maybe Joe felt Kell's instincts had lost their edge, Malone thought, and were dulled by his friendship with Montana Hodges.

Malone sat there silently after Clements left, reflecting on the things Joe had said. As much as it troubled him to admit it, the same doubts about Montana had crossed his mind earlier. He hadn't been able to forget the look in Sam Hinton's dying eyes after he was shot. His was not the normal look of a frightened, dying man, but one of bewilderment. Sam tried to say something to Montana—to ask him a question. Kell was sure of it. When he questioned Hodges about it, the man said nothing.

In addition, Montana had also witnessed the signing of the deed to his ranch. That knowledge had been gnawing at Kell's gut since his meeting with Sheriff Kimball. The young cowhand would never be a party to the cheating of a woman or the taking of her ranch—not the man Kell once knew.

Many things had happened since his return to Redhawk, things which made him question everything and everybody. Kell was beginning to think General Miles had been right, He *could* trust nobody. But maybe he was being too suspicious, Kell thought. At the same time, he refused to believe that was the case. There were just too many missing pieces, too many questions, and too little answers.

Malone was confident that Clay Adkins wanted him dead and was singlehandedly responsible for much of what happened. A chill went up his spine. Perhaps there were others . . .

While still turning the notion over in his head, a sweet, gentle voice interrupted his thoughts.

"Mr. Malone."

"What's that you say, Miss Payton?'

"I just asked what you wanted for breakfast."

"Nothing, ma'am. Just coffee would be fine."

"There's some pie in the kitchen," she said. "I just took it out of the oven."

"Fresh baked pie . . . huh? Don't guess I could turn that down, Miss Payton."

She returned from the kitchen carrying a large slab of apple pie. She set the plate down in front of him. Kell was still the only customer in the diner.

Nervously, she stood there for several seconds. The time seemed much longer to her. Rachel's mind was trying to form the words which suddenly became lost between her brain and her lips.

"May I sit down, Mr. Malone? There are some things I wanted to say to you."

Malone smiled. "I would be pleased if you did, Miss Payton," he said, rising to his feet as she sat down. "It isn't often I get to share a woman's company, let alone a handsome woman like you."

Rachel flushed at the statement.

"Man gets tired of looking at his horse," Malone continued. He tasted the pie. "This is really good, ma'am!"

"Thank you, Mr. Malone."

"Most of my friends call me Kell. I'd be proud to number you among them."

"Okay, Kell. But only if you call me Rachel. Miss Payton sounds like something you would call my grandmother." She smiled kind of sheepishly, always uncomfortable in Malone's presence. "I believe I owe you an apology. I said several unkind things to you yesterday and I'm sorry."

Malone held up his hand to stop her. "Apologies are only needed by the offended."

"You just wait a minute," Rachel said, her voice flaring. "I've finally worked up the courage to say this, Kell, so don't stop me until I'm through. You tried to warn me about Clay, but I wouldn't listen. Well, you were right. He's been acting strangely, ever since your return to town. And I think he's hiding something."

"I'm sorry to hear that . . . for your sake, I mean." Malone took another gulp of coffee. "But you already know what I think of him."

"Why do you hate him so?"

"Mostly, because it's so easy to do," Kell said with a smile. Then his face turned sober. "And I blame the man for my wife's death."

"Oh, come on! You don't really think he had anything to do with that, do you?"

"Not directly. But I believe he set in place a series of events that led up to it."

"I know Clay is not perfect, but I find that so hard to believe."

"There are three kinds of people in the world, Rachel. The first kind means you no harm. They have no desire to hurt anyone, but just want to be left alone. They will only retaliate in defense of themselves or others.

"The second group are made up of people who would harm you if given the chance. Fear is the only shackle which restrains them. They are fearful of punishment, retribution, or the arm of the law.

"Lastly, you have the unrestrained. These are the most dangerous. Oftentimes, their minds are distorted—some kind of flaw from the womb. Others are just naturally evil, obsessed with power and greed. They figure no one is big enough or tough enough to do whatever it takes to stop them. Murder and theft mean nothing to them, for they do not possess a conscience."

Kell tasted his coffee before continuing. "When a dog takes to killing chickens and develops a taste for blood, then the animal must be destroyed. Same goes for this crowd. The only thing that will permanently stop them is a bullet or a rope! Clay Adkins fits in this group."

"And what of you, Kellen Malone? You've killed some men, yourself . . . many of them, according to the reports. Which category do you fall under?"

Malone sat without speaking, carefully weighing the woman's question. "Strange as it may sound to you, I mean no living thing any harm. Sure, I've killed some men "I'm not denying that."

"How do you justify it?"

"I don't justify it, Rachel. I merely live with the consequences of it. As a young man, I was forced into a gun battle, one that couldn't be avoided. Fortunately, I came out on top. This earned me a reputation and brought new challenges from others. Guess I was just faster than most."

"Why don't you give it up and hang up your guns?"

"I can't. Don't you see? I wouldn't live ten minutes without a gun. Somebody would shoot me down in an alley, plant a gun in my hand. Probably, they'd say I drew first. Some young hothead is always trying to earn a name at my expense, ma'am. And I refuse to make it easy for them. You'll have to trust me on this, but it's hard to escape a reputation."

"How fast are you?"

"Not nearly as fast as some of those I buried."

Rachel looked bewildered. "I'm afraid I don't know what you mean. Why aren't you dead, if they were faster?"

"Speed is a relative thing, Rachel. A lot of men are fast with a gun, maybe the fastest in their town or area. The problem comes when they take in too much territory. Someone is always faster! Other factors come into play then."

"Other factors? What do you mean?"

"Has the man you're facing killed before? A man who has killed before will always be faster than someone who hasn't. A man who's never killed will hesitate to pull the trigger . . . not long, mind you. But it's much too long for a game where your life is wagered.

"A lot of men can draw and fire with some speed and accuracy. Not many can do it under pressure, in a stand-up fight or with someone shooting back at them. I can."

"Why do they do it then?"

"The fame, the notoriety—the reasons are many. The youngsters are the worst!"

"What do you mean?"

"There are a lot of kids out there, practicing with a six-gun, wanting to be the next Wes Hardin or something. Crazy as it sounds, every one of them thinks it glamorous and exciting. Trust me, Rachel, it isn't. I've seen men die. Many of them left behind grieving friends or loved ones.

150

Some of them left nothing but a bloody stain in the dirt to mark their passing.

"It takes a special kind of nerve or foolhardiness to look a man squarely in the eye, then to draw weapons against each other. One of you has to die, sometimes both. Some would call it courage, but I was thrust into many situations where there were no other choices."

"Couldn't you move to another place, change your name, and make a fresh start?"

"I wish it was that simple. I was a sheriff in Kansas for a couple of years, jailing drovers when they were drunk and disorderly. I pushed cows up any trail you care to name. And you already know about my time in Yuma. Sooner or later, someone would come along who recognized me. A man is never released from the prison of his past, Rachel. The bars are ones that we forge ourselves.

"I'd like nothing better than to walk away, but it's too late now. To hang up my guns is to invite death. And where does that leave Jesse? My ranch is here and Redhawk is my home. I'm not willing to give any of them up."

"I guess you've helped me to see things in a new light, Kell. However, I still don't profess to fully understand everything you've said."

"I didn't expect that you would."

"Kellen Malone, why do you always do that?" Rachel fumed.

"What?"

"You know what I mean . . . turning a polite conversation into an argument."

"Maybe you're just too sensitive," Kell said, his sober expression giving way to a grin.

She returned the smile. "My father used to do that," she explained, "making me smile even when I was angry with him. He was such a good man, Kell. Even when we disagreed, I still loved him. How I wish he were here!" the woman said. "Papa had so many dreams when he came west with me.

"He used to talk about the land, how wild and untamed it was. Papa said it was a place of wonder, violent as it was beautiful." A tear moistened her eye. "Why did he have to come here?"

"Tell me about what happened, Rachel."

"The Indians attacked the stage—Apaches—or so they said. There was a lot of shooting and Papa always believed in pulling his share of the load. Just as they started to flee, one of them fired another arrow. As fate would have it, the arrow struck him in the chest." She paused to gain her composure. "He died there in my arms. It was such a waste!"

"No, it wasn't, Rachel. Yes, it was a tragedy. I won't argue that. But from what you've told me, your father sounds like he was a proud man. This is the land he chose to put down roots. Your father died a free man, in the place of his choosing. A man can't ask anymore from life than that."

"Thank you, Kell." Rachel said, her eyes softening. "I'll think about what you said." She rose from her seat, smoothing down her apron as she stood. "Why is it you never talk about your wife, Kellen Malone?"

Kell paid her for the pie and coffee. "I don't know," he said with a shrug, as he started for the door. "Some things just shouldn't be dwelt on. And thanks for the pie. It was good."

Unwilling to let the matter drop, Rachel followed right behind him, like a dog yapping at his heels. "Tell me what Alice was like. Some people say I look just like her." Her eyes studied Malone, making him feel uncomfortable.

Kell knew he would have no peace until he answered her. "Alice was a handsome woman, Rachel. Never could understand why she took up with me. Kind and gentle she was, but there was some steel in her also.

And yes, you do look like her. But that isn't the only thing you and Alice have in common."

"What's that?"

Malone's face turned serious, with just the hint of a twinkle in his eye. "You see, she never learned to mind her own business either."

Rachel's face turned blood red. For a moment, Kell thought she would strike him.

"Kellen Malone," she fumed, "you are the most infuriating man I've ever met!"

Malone didn't let her say anything else. Kell quickly reached around her waist, drawing the woman to him. He kissed her firmly, yet softly. It was something he'd been considering since the first time they met. Rachel struggled at first, then yielded.

When they separated, no words passed between them. None were needed. From the way she returned his kiss, Kell believed her feelings to be the same as his. Malone went out the door and forked his horse. His lips whistled a tune while riding down the street.

Breathless, and with a hand touching her lips, Rachel watched Malone galloping away. Unexpectedly, the kiss had been given. Unwilling, she was not. Scared and strangely excited, Rachel knew what it meant to be truly in love. At the same time, a sense of guilt swept over her, realizing she had none of these same feelings for Clay Adkins.

As she stood there gawking in the doorway, a voice from behind startled her. "You care for him . . . no?" the cook said.

Rachel hadn't known he'd been standing there. Her face flushed with embarrassment.

Paco had been cooking at the diner for nearly two years. He was a man of medium height, nearly fifty-five years old. The apron he wore, stretched to its limit by a massive belly, carried the stains of his morning's labors. The cook's broken English was seasoned with a strong, Spanish accent.

"Yes, Paco. I care for him."

"I think Senor Malone is a good man."

She nodded.

"Senor Adkins is a very bad man, Rachel. Do not trust him. Sometimes Paco talk too much, but I live very long time. Learn many thing. You feel debt to Senor Adkins . . . what you call it?"

"Gratitude?"

"Si, gratitude. That is the word. Gratitude and love are not the same thing, senorita. Do not confuse them."

"Thank you for the advice, Paco."

"Do you help Paco now?" he asked with a grin. "Maybe you not done staring at empty street."

Rachel flushed again. "I'll be right there."

"Bueno," he replied. "I am no longer a young man and there is much work to be done."

Rachel laughed, as she heard him muttering to himself all the way back to the kitchen.

***

As Malone rode to the cemetery, he thought about Rachel and the feelings he had for her. For the first time since going to prison, he felt something besides hatred. Seven long years now behind him, hatred had been the kindling which fueled his will to survive. A woman never figured into his plans at all.

Thinking of Alice, Kell knew he should feel guilty, but it was not in him. Short as their time had been together, the bonds had been forged strongly. And a son had been born from that union. Malone felt sure that no matter where the bend in life's road might take him, Alice would be there always. And about Rachel . . . he knew she'd approve.

Drawing rein outside the solemn row of stones, Kell saw another horse tethered at the hitch rail. It quietly cropped the grass which sparsely grew around the posts. Taking a quick look at its flank, he could see it was wearing the brand of Clay Adkins.

Kell wondered what they were doing here. Slipping the thong off his six-gun, he quietly made his way through the rows. Every nerve was tensed, expecting an ambush. He then saw someone kneeling at one of the stones. From behind, something about the figure seemed strangely familiar. It was a feeling or a sense, not so much anything he could see.

Malone then saw the dog, resting on the ground beside the boy. The animal's ears perked up when he saw Kell, but he made no sound. Malone holstered his gun.

Quietly, like someone afraid to disturb the solitude of the place, Kell moved closer. Reading the name on the tombstone, his head dropped. The grave belonged to Alice.

The figure who knelt there then heard something behind him. He turned with a start, staring his father squarely in the eye. "Oh, it's you," he said, indifference in his tone.

Although it had been seven years, Malone recognized him immediately. He had grown to be a strapping youth, his once-yellow hair now as dark as his father's. Kell could see where some weight and muscle had been added to his frame, a product of age and hard work. One look would reveal he was a son to make any man proud.

"Hell, Jesse."

"I heard you were back. Never figured you'd show up here."

Malone wanted to throw his arms around the boy, to tell him how much he'd missed him. Now was not the time. Malone knew Clay had been right. Obviously, Jesse did blame Kell for his mother's death.

"Why do you say that?"

"I didn't think the infamous Kellen Malone cared for anyone," he said sarcastically. "Why bother yourself with remembering a dead woman?"

Kell ignored the comment. "Do you come here much? The place looks well kept, better than most of the others."

"Yeah, I try to keep it up. Hate to, though . . . graveyards still scare me a little."

"Except for the fact your ma is buried here, this ground is no more hallowed than anywhere else. Men have fallen all across this wide land of ours," Kell explained. "Many were buried where they fell, planted underneath the soil. Some were buried by the shifting sands. Anytime a man's foot strikes the earth, the chances are good that he has stepped on a gravesite."

"The whole country is a graveyard," Jesse recounted. "Yea, I remember you telling me that as a boy. It never did help much."

"We need to talk, Jesse."

"Why?" Jesse asked, turning his head away from his father. The time for talking has long since passed."

Kell walked around the boy. He squatted on his haunches in front of him, forcing Jesse to look him in the eye. "A lot of people have tried to keep me away from you, son. I don't know the reason for it. Words can't do you any harm. Maybe they're afraid of what I have to tell you. Maybe they're afraid you'll listen—afraid you'll learn the truth."

"The truth, you say? When did you care about honesty?"

Jesse tried to leave, but a firm hand on his shoulder kept him in place. "I've got something to tell you, Jesse. And you're dead sure going to listen!"

"There's nothing you can say that I'd be interested in hearing. You killed Ma!"

"I know you blame me for your mother's death. Well, why shouldn't you?" Kell hung his head. "I blame myself every day. If I hadn't gone to prison, Alice might still be alive. I know that. But there's one thing you have to know . . . I didn't rob that stage."

Although it was still early in the day, the sun was blistering. Kell took off his hat, ran the back of his hand across his brow, and then returned the hat to his head.

"I loved your mother, son. I loved her more than anything. The only thing that comes close is my feelings for you. Sheriff Kimball and I have a couple of hunches about who held up the stage and why they did it. They're the ones you ought to hate—not me!"

Malone saw something in Jesse's eyes which made him think he believed the story—or wanted to believe it. The expression faded quickly, leaving only the contempt.

"Why should I believe you," Jesse asked. "Why should anyone?"

"I don't know, son. Maybe I was fool enough to think you'd want to believe your pa. Maybe I thought you'd trust your ma's instincts. Alice ever tell you I'd done anything wrong? Tell me, boy . . . did she?"

Jesse shook his head, but said nothing. His mother had always believed in Kell's innocence. He knew that to be the truth.

"When did she sell the ranch, Jesse?"

"Sell the ranch?" he blustered. "Ma never sold the ranch to anyone! She said it was the one part of you she was holding on to."

"Somebody's got you fooled, son. Clay Adkins has a deed to the place—the sheriff's seen it! Clay said he bought it from your mother." Kell could see the news came as a shock to him. "What's the matter, boy? You look bee stung. Didn't Clay ever tell you that?"

Jesse couldn't bring himself to admit that his father might be right. "I don't care what he's got. Ma went pretty fast after the horse kicked her."

Now, Malone was stunned. "You mean she didn't die of the fever?"

"No, whatever gave you that idea?"

"That's what Montana said in his letter."

The anger rose in his eyes. "Montana . . . huh? I've heard just about enough of this. Should've known a thief couldn't stick to the truth." He shook his head. "You are good . . . I'll have to give you that. You almost had me believing you." Jesse got up to leave. This time, Kell made no attempt to stop him from going.

"Jesse, one other thing . . ."

The young man paused, with his back still turned towards Malone.

"There are some questions you'd better ask yourself, boy. Who stands to benefit by getting me out of the way? Why did two men try to kill me yesterday? Why did someone shoot at me today?" He hesitated before the last question. "Most of all, why is Montana named as a witness on Clay's deed to our ranch?

"You come up with an answer to those questions, Jesse. If you do, it'll give you some idea as to the ones really responsible for your ma's death."

"All right, you've had your say. Now I've got a question for you," he said bitterly. "Why didn't you ever write to me?"

There was no hesitation in Kell's answer. "I did, Jesse . . . all the time."

The boy said nothing further as he and Lobo walked away.

Chapter Ten

"What did he say to you, Jesse?" Rachel asked. "He must have said something."

Lobo contentedly lay on a rug next to the hearth, gently wagging his tail from time to time. Exhausted from his game with Jesse, the dog chewed on the tooth-marked, wooden mop handle.

"He said a lot of things, Miss Rachel. Some of them made a lot of sense. The others left me more confused. I just don't know. He's been gone so long. Now he comes back into my life, casting suspicions on the people I know . . . people I trust. He's sure asking a lot of me."

"A father has a right to ask a lot of his son."

"I reckon that's so," he admitted, slouching against the wall. "But he ain't been much of a father."

"Circumstances didn't give him much of a chance."

Jesse's voice flared. "Nobody made him rob that stage."

"Why don't you give him the benefit of the doubt, Jesse?" she softly pleaded. "I think he deserves that much."

Although Rachel had chosen to cast her lot with Malone's innocence, she appreciated the dilemma which Jesse faced. He was still a boy—a good boy—forced to make a man-sized decision.

"If I believe his story, then I'll be forced to go against the word of some others."

"You mean Clay?"

"Yes. Miss Rachel. Clay hasn't ever given me any reason to distrust him. Kellen Malone is nearly a stranger to me, just some memory from my past." The boy gently scratched his dog's ears. He's just someone who played with us when we were younger. You think that should buy him any special favors?

"Clay didn't even want me talking to him. Said he's fill my head with lies. Clay even kept me out of school, just to make it hard for him to find me. It was just chance we ran into each other today."

"Kind of strange, isn't it? Alice brought you two back together, even after she was gone. It sounds like fate to me."

Nervously, Jesse paced the room. "What do you think I ought to do, Miss Rachel?"

She pondered over the question before answering. "That is something only you can answer. It's not my place to tell you what to do. My mind is already made up about your father."

"You care for him, don't you?"

"Yes, I do, Jesse."

"I thought so. Every time Pa's name is mentioned, I can see it in your eyes."

"Did you hear yourself, Jesse? You just called him "Pa" for the first time."

Jesse shook his head. "I reckon he'll always be that, no matter whether I believe him or not. I just don't know what to think anymore."

"I'm not a very old person, Jesse, but I have learned to follow my heart in such matters. It will seldom steer you wrong. What is your heart telling you to do?"

"I want to believe him."

"Then do it."

"You make it sound so easy, Miss Rachel. I wish it was that simple. Thanks for talking to me anyway," the boy uttered. "Come on, Lobo. We'll go see Montana."

The scraggly, black dog followed him to the door, still carrying the stick. "Leave that thing here, Lobo. There won't be any more time to play this afternoon." The dog dropped the stick to the floor.

Rachel followed them as out the door as they left. "You'll be back in time for dinner, won't you?"

Jesse swung into the saddle. "Yes, ma'am. I'll be here."

"Remember, Jesse. Follow your heart."

Her talk with Jesse also made it clear that Rachel could no longer continue living in a house claimed by her fiancé, as long as she was in love with another man. She knew that she would have to find another place to live. Tomorrow, she would pack her things and have a talk with Clay. She knew it would be difficult conversation for both of them.

Rachel watched as Jesse disappeared over the hill with the dog still following him. A chill came over her suddenly. But she could not explain the feeling.

***

The broiling, midday sun had climbed high in the cloudless, Arizona sky. Nervously, the man watched it through the upstairs hotel window, conscious that the stage would be arriving in Redhawk soon.

He furiously ransacked the chest of drawers, throwing all the belongings onto the bed. These he hurriedly stuffed into a newly-purchased carpetbag. A fly buzzed in the room, a horse stamped its foot outside, and he was conscious of every sound. Sweat trickled down the man's forehead, perspiration that had little to do with the heat. The man was sweating out of fear.

Clay Adkins mopped his forehead with a handkerchief. He checked his watch, checked it again, and then spied another look out the corner of the window.

Adkins realized there was not much time left. The stage would be arriving in town soon. He planned to be on it. Adkins knew his life depended on his immediate departure from Redhawk. And with life, there was always an opportunity for revenge.

So busy was the man with his packing, he failed to see the wiry, young cowhand who ambled up the street towards the hotel.

Like a ball of twine left to the cat, all his plans had gone awry. Nothing was left anymore—nothing but the ticket in his coat pocket and the dreams of what might have been. Clay continued packing, because he knew the time was short.

He regretted there had been no time to express his "goodbyes" to Rachel. Perhaps he could wire her from another town. Maybe she would join him. And even if she didn't, Miss Payton was simply one woman in a land of many. He would be alive.

Adkins blamed Kellen Malone for his misfortune. He'd almost killed the man earlier that morning, when he staked out the road with a rifle. Clay cursed the man's good luck. Yet he consoled himself with one thought . . . the man wouldn't be alive to see dawn. Stadler and Hodges would see to that. And Clay had no intention of allowing the same fate to befall himself.

With Malone out of the picture, Adkins would deal with the other two later . . . from less hazardous surroundings. Then he would return to Redhawk to start fresh. He laughed to himself. "My plans are not destroyed, merely postponed," he mumbled, just under his breath.

Although Clements had taken his money without killing Malone, he felt no animosity towards the skull-faced gunman. Had the situation been reversed, it was exactly the kind of thing he would have done. And besides, Skull had warned him of Stadler's plans and Montana's betrayal. His life, he figured, was worth considerably more than five thousand dollars.

Shoving the last of his clothes into the bag, Adkins smiled as he heard the team of horses thundering down the street. He was going to make it. In a few minutes, he'd be riding a stage bound for Nevada. No one could hurt him there.

"Goodbye, you fools!" he said with a smile.

As Adkins opened the door to his hotel room, he immediately saw a tall figure blocking the doorway.

Clay's heart sank . . .

***

As his horse slipped into Redhawk, Jesse Malone checked the position of the sun. The boy saw it was around one o'clock, the stage's arrival eliminating all doubt.

Tipping his hat to the one handling the reins, Jesse continued up the street, still hoping to find his friend, Montana. Many of the townspeople were out on the street, hurriedly going about their business. Yet he didn't see the good-natured cowhand anywhere among them.

"We've got to find Montana," Jesse said to the dog. "He'll know what I should do."

Finally, he spied his friend going up the street, walking into the hotel. Jesse called after him, but in the commotion, Montana heard nothing.

"Lobo, you wait here," ordered the boy. "I'll be right back." The dog wagged his tail and sat down outside the hotel.

Tying a knot around the hitching rail, Jesse went inside. The hotel clerk directed him to look upstairs for his friend.

***

Adkins found himself staring into the eyes of Montana Hodges and down the barrel of the young man's gun.

"Going somewhere, Clay?" he muttered sarcastically. "I see you've been talking to Skull Clements. He must have warned you, didn't he?" Hodges feigned a look of disappointment. "Never figured the man for a talker."

"Yes, he came and talked to me, Mr. Hodges. No matter what else the man is, Skull Clements is loyal. But I don't suppose you would know anything about that quality."

"Ain't you gonna invite me in?"

Adkins backed away from the door, wishing his right hand wasn't holding the carpetbag. Sweat was trickling down his forehead again.

Montana walked into the room, using his heel to kick the door closed. "Now that's more like it, Clay. And I thought you wasn't going to be very neighborly."

"I expected this sort of thing from Stadler, but never from you. How stupid I've been! I was foolish to trust a man who betrayed his own best friend. It's the woman, isn't it?"

"No, Clay. Miss Payton has nothing to do with it."

Clay's mind was racing, trying to figure a way out. "Deke and Julio were waiting outside, Montana. How did you get by them?"

"There's no one out there, Clay. You're on your own," Montana said with a laugh. "I always gave you credit for some brains. Guess I was wrong. Deke and Julio . . . Stadler owns them too. After a serious discussion about your short future, it wasn't hard to persuade them.

"Stadler thought you might be planning a little trip. Said I should give you a little something to remember him by. You might call it a token of his affection."

"You don't have to do this," pleaded Clay, his eyes gripped in fear. "We could work something out between ourselves."

"I had to make a choice, Clay—you or Stadler. It seemed safer working for him. You do know the man's crazy, don't you?"

Adkins gently began to ease the carpetbag towards the floor, hoping to free his gunhand.

"Be careful, Clay!" he said, motioning at him with the gun. "I'm liable to think you might be going for a gun. I know you ain't in no hurry to die."

"Why are you doing this, Montana?"

"Only four people know about the stage hold-up: Deke Hinton, Stadler, you, and I. With you dead, it only leaves three. Stadler won't talk and Deke can't afford to. Besides, Stadler knows all about the woman. I don't know how he found out about Alice, but he did. He threatened to expose me if I didn't help him."

"You're a fool!"

"That's funny, Clay. I'm the one holding all the cards . . . and the gun."

"You're wrong, Montana! Carlton Stadler is holding all the cards. You're just one of the chips he is playing . . . like I am. When he grows bored with the game, he'll cast you aside, also. He'll probably kill you or see that you hang. It just depends on whichever provides him the most entertainment."

"You side with me, Montana, and I'll give you anything you want. You want money . . . I'll get it for you." Adkins was desperate. "I'll even let you have the woman. You've seen Rachel . . . beautiful, isn't she? She looks just like Alice Malone. You can have her!"

"Good try, Clay, but it's no deal. I've had my fill of women . . . brought me nothing but trouble." Montana leveled the gun at the man's chest and motioned towards the door. "You're going to walk down the back stairs ahead of me, Clay. I wish it didn't have to be this way. I'd hoped that Kell would kill you and make things easy on me. Now, start walking. And don't make a peep!"

Adkins no longer brooded over his failed plans; he gave no further thought to revenge. Clay only wanted to live. "You think you're so smart, don't you? You think you know everything, Montana. You don't! You don't have any idea who Stadler really is. No one does."

"What are you talking about, Clay?" Hodges was skeptical. "This wouldn't be another stall for time, would it?"

"This is no stall, you fool! Does the name Tom Candrey mean anything to you?"

Montana nodded. "Everyone's heard of Candrey. Not many know what he looks like. You're not saying . . .?"

"That's precisely what I'm saying . . . Carlton Stadler is Tom Candrey! I've known it for some time now."

Momentarily shaken by this latest news, Montana quickly regained his composure. "This changes nothing, you know. Just makes it more dangerous for me to cross the man. But thanks for the information." He gestured towards the door with the revolver. "Come on, Clay. Let's get going."

At that moment, the door burst open. "I've been looking all over for you, Montana," Jesse exclaimed.

Hodges, distracted by the boy's sudden interruption, turned to look behind him.

Adkins saw Jesse's arrival as the chance he had been seeking. Clay figured to get no others. Dropping the bag from his hand, Clay's hand went for his gun. Although the draw had been swift and unexpected, he found himself no match for the speed of the young cowhand.

Montana wheeled back around, an ugly sneer on his lips, the six-gun coming level as he turned. The gun flamed in his hand, as two .44 slugs passed each other in flight. But only one of them found its target.

Clay's bullet went wide of Montana, tearing its way through the paper-thin walls. Adkins was not so lucky, as Montana's heavy slug pierced his right lung. Clay willed himself to fire again, but could not. Adkins coughed, blood frothing from his mouth.

Montana coldly triggered his gun again, erasing any remaining vestige of life from his victim. Adkins slumped over on the floor, cold and still, a candidate for Perdition. On the floor beside him, there lay a blood-stained ticket to the stage.

At the first sign of shooting, Jesse had thrown himself to the floor. Hearing the guns stilled, he pushed past Hodges, and knelt beside Clay.

"He's dead, Montana," the boy said, his eyes wide with fear. It was his first encounter with death. "You killed him!"

"I had to, Jesse. He drew on me first." A strange look came to his face. "How long were you outside that door?"

Jesse had never seen Montana this way. The cowhand looked at him accusingly, his eyes wild with rage and fear.

"Not very long."

Hodges pointed the gun at Jesse and motioned towards the door. "I can't take any chances. Now, come with me."

As Jesse came to his feet, he heard someone running up the stairs towards them. It was Sheriff Bill Kimball.

Without any warning, Montana brought the gun to bear on the sheriff. He squeezed off two quick shots. Kimball grunted hard, clutching at his chest. The gun fell from his fingers and clattered on the floor. Sheriff Kimball staggered backwards, tumbling down the steps. His body came to rest in a blood-stained heap at the foot of the staircase.

Jesse, sensing he had stumbled into a situation he knew nothing about, seized the opportunity to escape. Seeing the window, the boy flung himself headlong outside. Glass shattered in all directions. Scrambling to his feet, Jesse ran down the roof, and jumped to the street.

As Hodges saw Jesse escaping, his first impulse was to catch the boy. But fully aware that Kellen Malone was his main concern, Montana made no effort to give chase. There would be plenty of time for that later. As Hodges came down the steps, he coldly stepped over the sheriff's fallen body, offering the same respect he might have given a dead rattlesnake.

The boy raced for his horse, his mind still reeling from the event he had just witnessed. Lobo waited for him there.

Montana a killer . . . the thought seemed almost foreign to him. But Jesse knew he must get away from there. He had to find a place to hide—a place to think. He knew just the place. Jesse rammed the horse in the flanks and it promptly bolted out of town.

The dog followed along behind.

***

A pair of hard-bitten outlaws waited at the spring, on the back of Malone's ranch. Despicable as they were dangerous, the two gave as little thought to murder and larceny as a rancher did to tending his stock. Their killing trail had been a long one, circumvented by none, stained with the blood of many.

Deke Hinton and Julio knew Kellen Malone would return to this spot. Adkins had tipped them to the location, something he learned from talking to Rachel. They had since found traces of his campfire and the prints of his horse. To kill him, they had only to wait for his return.

"Maybe he won't come," Julio said, chewing on a piece of jerked meat. "It'll be dark in a couple of hours."

"He'll be here," Deke affirmed. "Adkins said the woman saw a fire up here last night. It had to be him."

"I wish we had one," the Mexican said between bites. "Do you think they kill Adkins?"

"I figure so . . . Montana was going to take care of it. I don't like double-crossing a man, but Stadler ain't exactly the kind of man you argue with." Hinton rubbed his hands together, trying to warm them. "You never told me. Why do they just call you Julio? Ain't you got a last name?"

"My mother was a woman of little virtue, Senor. My father was never known to me."

The outlaw laughed. "I'd have liked to know your mother. Sounds like she might have been a lot of fun."

The Mexican's dark eyes glared at his partner. "You talk too much, Hinton. Maybe you end up dead."

"Could be," Deke said with a chuckle. "Could be."

Neither of them spoke for a time. Julio ended the silence. "I think I hear something." The two of them sat quietly, guns drawn and cocked.

A hoof rattled against a stone. "I think you're right, Amigo. Somebody's coming."

As the two outlaws watched from cover, they saw a figure coming up the trail. "Looky here," spoke Deke, quietly. He nudged Julio in the arm. "Here comes Malone's kid."

"Are you sure?"

"Yea, that's him. I never figured on this, Julio. A man can catch anything if he tosses out the right kind of bait. As long as we have the boy, Malone will have to come for him."

The Mexican grinned. "You think good . . . for a gringo. If you find the cub, can the bear be far behind?"

The two of them shared a quiet laugh.

As Jesse's horse drew near to the outlaws' location, a loop settled around his shoulders. The boy struggled against the rope, but he knew it was futile. Hinton pulled hard on the rope, jerking him from the saddle. With no way to catch himself, the boy slammed to the ground.

The outlaw, Hinton, smiled viciously as he tugged on the lariat. "Roped, throwed, and about to be branded."

Quickly returning to his senses after the fall, Jesse yelled, "Lobo! Help!"

The fierce black dog, ever loyal to his friends, charged from behind the rocks. The look of the devil in his eyes, Lobo barked and leaped at Hinton. The dog's teeth clamped onto the man's leg like a steel trap. He struck and tore at the man, pulling huge chunks of flesh from his chest, arms, and back.

The outlaw rolled over and over on the ground, using his arms to shield his head and neck. The animal innately sensed the neck is a vulnerable place, one that would bring a quick end to his friend's adversary.

Deke screamed like a wounded animal, desperately fighting for his life, wrestling to get free of the black, snarling creature. Finally, Hinton reached his gun. He slashed down at the dog with the barrel, freeing himself momentarily.

The Mexican, who had been powerless to help, now saw his chance to do something. Julio palmed his gun, triggering three quick shots at the dog. Lobo yelped loudly, grazed by one of the slugs. The dog raced into the rocks for safety.

Jesse tugged at the rope and tried to free himself. When he came to his feet, Julio turned the gun on him. "Try to run," he said, "and I kill you!"

Hinton tried to stand, staggering once before he could get to his feet. His shirt was hanging in shreds, his wounds dripping blood. Curses rang from his mouth like gunfire during a shootout. He ran over to the boy and backhanded him into unconsciousness. Wildly, he eared back the hammer of his six-gun, taking aim at Jesse's head. "I'm gonna kill you! You . . .! Hinton started to take up slack in the trigger.

"Don't!" Julio screamed. "We need him . . . for now."

"Okay! Okay! You're right, Mex. I'll let it go . . . for now." Hinton let back the hammer grudgingly, scarcely concerned whether the gun fired or not.

The two outlaws then bound the boy hand and foot. They also gagged him. After dragging the unconscious boy back into the rocks, they tried to erase any signs of their presence. Then Julio did his best to clean and dress Hinton's wounds.

After that, they waited . . .

A couple of hours later, Jesse awoke to the sounds of conversation. One of the voices sounded remarkably familiar to him.

It was Montana Hodges.

The boy lay there silently, feigning unconsciousness.

"Any sign of him?" Julio asked.

"No, nothing yet," said Deke, who was still hurting from his wounds.

"Will you two keep your voices down?" Montana growled irritably. "You want to scare him off?"

"He won't go anywhere," Julio observed, "not as long as we have the young one."

"I thought you wanted us to handle it," Hinton grumbled. "What's the matter? Don't you trust us?"

Julio glared at Hodges also, still waiting for an answer to Deke's question.

"Stadler wanted me to make sure this was done right." He threw a nod in Hinton's direction. "From the look of things, you need my help. Letting a dog chew on you . . . how stupid can you get!"

As Montana stared at the seemingly still figure of the boy, his eyes softened. "It's too bad he couldn't have been mine, you know. Jesse's been like a son to me. His pa and I used to be real good friends at one time. Real close we were!"

"Some friend, you are!" Hinton muttered. "Tried to steal Malone's woman while he was away at prison. Yeah, I'd love having a friend like you."

Jesse couldn't believe his ears. He recalled the young cowhand spending a lot of time out at the ranch, but he always thought Montana was just being kind to them. He wondered how he could have been so blind. He then remembered that his mother always seemed less than happy about Montana's increasingly frequent visits. Jesse never under-stood it at the time.

Angered by Hinton's comment, Montana pulled his gun. "I'm going to kill you, Deke!"

Julio placed a hand on his arm. "Not now. Malone might hear the shot."

"You're right, Julio." Hodges gently released the hammer. "Just as soon as we get Kell, I'm going back to Redhawk."

Hinton's face was pale and he pulled a blanket around himself. "Sounds to me like you're getting soft, Hodges. Maybe you're losing your nerve."

Montana glared at him coldly, the young cowhand's eyes throwing daggers from under the brim of his hat. "If you keep talking, Deke, you're going to lose a lot more than that! Maybe you should learn to keep your mouth shut."

"I told him the same thing, Senor Hodges."

"Well, I've kept our little secret for seven years now . . . me and Sam," Hinton muttered. "Nobody ever found out about the stage robbery and our part in it."

"That doesn't make any difference, Deke. Stadler doesn't like loud-mouths; I don't like them either. A loose tongue could buy you a six foot parcel of sod."

Hinton glared at Montana. "I'll keep it in mind."

"You'd better!"

"Where do you think he is, Senor Hodges? It will be dark soon."

"Don't fret about it, Julio. He'll be along."

Chapter Eleven

Kellen Malone knelt along the trail, studying the tracks. He'd spent most of the afternoon searching and his determination had finally been rewarded. Finally, he located the place where the Chiricahuas were crossing into Mexico.

As he studied the signs there before him, something else caught his eye. The Apaches had met up with a white man at this spot. Kell eyed the track for a long time, refusing to believe what he was seeing. He immediately recognized the print. Malone scooped up a handful of dust, throwing it to the ground in disgust. He swore softly.

The track belonged to Montana's horse.

"Doggone you, Montana!" Kell grumbled. "Why did you have to get involved in this mess anyhow?"

Just then, he heard the hoof falls of another rider. Malone stood to his feet and walked over to his horse. As the rider approached him, Kell deliberately positioned the animal between himself and the stranger. His finger gently loosed the thong from the hammer.

Kell studied the man carefully. He could see the stranger was dressed much the same as any other drifting cowhand, but something about the man didn't ring true. His clothes didn't show enough wear to be a drover. Malone was suspicious.

As the stranger drew closer, Kell pegged him to be a young man, scarcely in his early twenties. He also noticed the rider was sporting little, if any, growth of beard, indicating that the young man had shaved sometime recently. He doubted the stranger was an outlaw though. Men on the run seldom concern themselves with proper grooming.

Stumbling upon him like this, Kell figured it had to be more than a coincidence that he was here. And if this stranger was involved in trading liquor to the Apaches, being found in this spot could cost Malone his life. Warily, Kell watched every movement.

"Howdy, neighbor," the man said, drawing rein twenty feet in front of the tracks. "Couldn't help but notice you down here. You tracking someone?"

There was nothing Malone disliked more than a meddler. "You always been this nosy, kid? Or could it be that you're fishing for something in particular?"

"Didn't mean any harm, mister. The name is Denton Turner. Most folks call me Dent." The man stepped down from his horse.

"How do you do, Dent?" Kell replied. He didn't offer his hand and he was still using the horse for cover. Malone wondered if there were any others with him.

"You got a name, friend?"

"I sure do," Kell said. "Had one every since I was a boy." Having said that, Malone made no other reply.

Turner studied him for a time before speaking. He hadn't missed the fact that Malone was using the horse for a shield.

"You're not very talkative, friend."

"I reckon you're right," Malone said with a straight face. "Always been a fault of mine." Kell thought he detected a hint of anger in the man's eyes. The idea pleased him. It occurred to him that young Mr. Turner was not accustomed to insolence.

"I've been riding for quite a spell," Turner explained. "You're the first man I've seen in some time."

"Lots of folk in Redhawk! Surprised you didn't see any of them, seeing as how you just came from that direction."

The stranger knew he'd been caught. Turner did his best to hide it. "That's too bad," he replied. "Must have just missed it somehow."

Malone could see the man was lying. "Only one good reason a long-riding man would avoid a town. You on the dodge, kid?"

"No sir. I'm not running from the law."

The only thing that Kell hated worse than a meddler was a liar.

"Then you are a liar!" Malone deliberately stepped out from behind the horse when he spoke. "You couldn't have missed the town by accident, Mr. Turner. Now, what is your business here on my ranch? And your answer better be a good one! My patience is wearing thin."

Denton Turner put both hands in the air, so there could be no mistaking his intentions. He took one more look around to make sure they were still alone.

"You must be Mr. Kellen Malone."

Kell eyed him strangely. "And what if I am?"

"Then I am pleased to make you acquaintance." The man then tipped his hat. "I am Sergeant Denton Turner, assigned to General Nelson Miles."

"How do I know you're who you say you are, Sergeant?"

"General Miles said you'd ask about that. He told me to tell you that he still considered Custer a fool."

Malone smiled, stepping forward to offer his hand. "Pleased to meet you, sergeant."

"The pleasure is all mine, Mr. Malone. Your heroics with the Michigan Brigade are nothing short of legendary." He pumped Kell's hand. "And just call me Dent until this thing is over. Don't want folks knowing I'm with the military. Might make them freer to talk." The sergeant was all business. "What have you learned so far?"

"Not too much, really. This is where the Chiricahuas are crossing the border. They met a wagon here." Malone walked along, pointing at the ground. "See those tracks, Dent. The wagon doesn't cut so deep when they leave. Looks like those Apaches didn't ride away empty handed.

The traders must have dealt them something." Kell smiled knowingly. "Any guesses what it might have been?"

"Whiskey," Dent replied.

"That and probably a few rifles."

"You recognize any of the tracks, Malone?"

Kell was hesitant to answer. "Yes, I do." Kell squatted on his haunches, pointing at one set of hoof prints. "This horse is being ridden by Montana Hodges."

A student of human nature, Denton Turner immediately sensed Malone's reluctance to respond. "This Hodges, is he a friend of yours?"

"A good friend . . . or he used to be." Kell looked at the young soldier with new eyes. "You don't miss much . . . do you, Mr. Turner?"

"I try to be observant, sir," Denton smiled. "Good trait for a soldier. Don't you think?"

Malone nodded.

Turner's mind never drifted too far outside the realm of his duties. "You're a former military man, Mr. Malone. What's your evaluation of the situation?"

"I don't think Hodges is the man you're looking for, Dent. Somebody bigger than him is running things. True, he's part of this somehow, but Montana is just small potatoes. The big spud is still out there."

"You think it's Clay Adkins?"

"He'd get my vote."

"Then let's head for Redhawk, Mr. Malone."

"Before you start sounding the attack, Sergeant, there's one other wild card in this game. His name is Carlton Stadler. I think the man isn't what he seems.

Turner was familiar with the name. "Isn't he the lawyer who defended you?"

"If that's what you want to call it."

Although they had gotten off to a bad start, Denton warmed to Kell quickly. There was an undeniable honesty to the man which Turner admired. Then there was his war record. Turner respected Malone's exploits long before they ever had the chance to meet. The sergeant didn't for one minute believe the man was, or ever had been a criminal.

Turner's face turned somber. "I'm sorry about your friend, Mr. Malone. You know I'll have to take him in, don't you?"

"Yea, I know it." Malone forked his saddle, his eyes studying the sergeant. "You any good with that hogleg?"

"I'm a fair shot. Why are you asking?"

"How fast can you get into action?"

Turner was puzzled. "I've never been too much for speed, but fast guns are often overrated."

"Not this one, Sergeant. I've seen Montana Hodges in action and few men are a match for him. If you don't mind, I'll be the one to tell him."

"I'm not afraid of your friend!" said Turner, his pride hurting from what he considered to be a deliberate slight. He mounted his horse.

"You misunderstand me Sergeant." His smile put the officer at ease. "I'm not questioning your courage. There's not one doubt in my mind that you've got the grit to face Hodges. I'm just offering my help, if you'll have it."

Turner returned the smile. "If you put it that way, I'd be much obliged."

The two of them started their horses down the trail for Redhawk.

***

Rachel watched the evening sun, as it gently dipped below the face of the mountaintops. Nervously, she scanned the horizon, hoping to see more than the beauty of another sunset. Her hopes were lifted as she saw a pair of riders come into view.

"Mr. Halstead," she yelled. "Somebody's coming."

Buck Halstead, concerned about the safely of his nephew, had ridden out to the ranch to look for Jesse. Upon his arrival, he discovered the boy had not returned. The events of the day and the fact that Jesse was still missing had them both worried. Moreover, Kellen Malone was nowhere to be found either. Halstead was busily hitching up a buckboard so that he and Rachel could go out in search of the young man.

"I see them now, Miss Payton," he said, walking out beside her. In his hands he carried a double barrel shotgun.

As he approached the ranch, he saw Rachel standing there looking towards the horizon. Then he saw a big man with a shotgun take his place beside her. His first thought was that the man was Clay Adkins, but closer inspection revealed it to be Buck.

Riding closer, Kell could see the welcome in her eyes and a smile. But something in her countenance dropped when she saw the face of the other rider. Malone dismounted before the horse came to a stop.

Bewildered, Kell looked at Halstead. "Evening, Buck. What brings you out this way?"

Rachel ran towards him, threw her arms around him, and began to weep on Kell's shoulder. "I'm so glad to see you, but I hoped you found Jesse."

"No, Rachel. He's not with me. I figured he was here." Kell motioned at the other rider. "Buck, Rachel, this is Denton Turner."

Buck walked over and shook his hand. Rachel smiled politely, as Dent tipped his hat to her. "Pleased to meet you, ma'am."

"You're trembling, Rachel," Kell said. "What is it? What's happened, Buck?"

"You don't know?" she said, with a look of surprise.

"Know what? Will somebody please tell me what's going on here?"

"Kell, there was a shooting in town today," Buck said.

Rachel interrupted him. "Montana shot Clay . . . he's dead!"

"Montana?"

She nodded.

Kell pulled her closer to him. "I'm so sorry, Rachel. I know how you felt about him. How are you holding up?"

"Oh, I'm all right." Rachel's eyes betrayed her. "The whole thing came as a shock. I cared for him very much at one time, until I found out about the lies. Now that he's dead, I feel so guilty about everything."

"There's no reason to."

"I know you never liked him, Kell, but Clay and I were to be married. I even had my wedding dress ready. How could I have been so wrong about him?"

"Don't be so hard on yourself, Rachel." Malone lightly stroked her cheek. "You're not the one with poor judgment. Montana Hodges is my friend. But now I'm sure he let me go to prison for a crime he himself committed."

"Are you sure?" Buck asked.

"Unless I miss my guess, I think Montana and the Hinton brothers robbed that stage seven years ago. It's the only explanation that makes sense." Kell turned away from Buck and stared deeply into Rachel's eyes. "And if you'll forgive me for saying so, Clay Adkins was involved in the robbery too. Carlton Stadler had some knowledge of it later, I think."

"It sounds like you're talking conspiracy, Kell," Buck offered.

"That's exactly what I'm saying. Adkins was after the ranch and Stadler was paid to lose my trial." He pushed the hat back on his head. "I can't get a handle on how Montana figures into all of this. There's a piece missing somewhere. Did Kimball go after Hodges?"

"No, he didn't," Buck said. "After Montana killed Clay, the sheriff tried to arrest him. Montana shot Kimball too."

"Will he make it?"

"The doctor says it's too early to tell," Rachel replied, wiping away a tear. "He'll probably be all right if he makes it until morning."

"Before he lost consciousness, Skull Clements was there with him," Buck added. "After Clements agreed to do it, Kimball deputized him right there on the spot. The idea didn't sit real well with a lot of the townspeople."

"Where's Joe now?'

"He's out tracking Montana. He left as soon as he pinned on the badge."

Malone turned to go. "He'll probably need some help."

"Wait, Kell!" Rachel said. "There's more you don't know."

Arrested by something in the woman's voice, Malone stopped. Looking from one to the other, Kell could see the fear reflected in their expressions.

"After Montana killed Clay, someone was seen fleeing out the window of his room. The witnesses said it was a boy . . . a boy followed by a black dog."

"You mean it was Jesse?"

"I'm afraid so," Rachel said, wiping away a tear. "Jesse was supposed to join me for dinner this evening. He never made it. When I heard about the shooting, I hoped he was with you. Mr. Halstead and I were just getting ready to go look for him."

"Don't you worry your pretty little head over Jesse. I'll find him, Rachel."

"I'll go with you," Halstead replied.

"No, Buck. I want you to stay here. Montana's still on the loose. Wouldn't want Rachel alone if he showed up here."

"Okay, Kell."

"Dent, Hodges will have to wait. I have to find Jesse first," he said, checking the loads on both his six-guns. "You mind staying here too?"

180

"No problem, Malone. I have to take care of a couple of things in town first. Then I will come right back." Once more, Turner tipped his hat to the lady and started his horse on the road to Redhawk.

"Kell, please be careful," Rachel said. "I don't want anything to happen to you or Jesse."

"I'll be all right. So will Jesse." Kell drew her close, kissing her gently. The words he would say took her by surprise. "I love you, Rachel Payton."

Kell forked his saddle. "Jesse is looking for a place to hide and I think I might know where he's gone." He did his best to calm the woman's fears. "Jesse is a smart boy and he has Lobo with him. He'll be okay. You go on back in the house now. We'll be along a little later."

Rachel watched in silence as Malone rode towards the mountain. She feared that this might be the last time.

***

As the outlaws talked, they were unaware that Jesse Malone was hanging on their every word. Had they known, the boy's spying would have given them little cause for concern. They had no intention of ever letting him escape anyway. Dead children can be seen and not heard. Jesse had been bound and gagged, his fate waiting for the final card to be dealt.

Kell's son now knew the truth about the stage robbery. He also learned the grim truth about the man who had once been his friend. The knowledge left him cold, empty, and betrayed. At the same time, Jesse felt ashamed. His father had been telling him the truth all along, yet he had doubted the man's word.

For the first time, the boy developed a new understanding and appreciation of the woman who gave him birth. Also, he could never forget her stubborn insistence as to her husband's innocence. Unlike her son, Alice Malone had been right about him from the very beginning.

He also better understood the man, Kellen Malone, who he had spent so much time trying to hate. Jesse regretted all the cruel thoughts which had come to his mind, the unkind words he had spoken. The boy longed to set things right . . . but he doubted it would ever happen. If these men had their way, then there would be little time for either of them—the father and the son.

Wishing his father was there with him, yet glad he wasn't, Jesse plotted his plans to escape. Calling on every bit of knowledge he received as a boy, his mind still came up empty. Lobo was hurt—maybe dead. Therefore, he could count on no more help from the dog.

Think! That is what he must do, Jesse told himself. Pa always said there was a solution to every problem, a way out of every situation. Man had only to think.

Jesse realized the outlaws had staked out the only possible trail leading to the mountaintop and were waiting to ambush his father. It was likely he would come soon and Jesse must find a way to warn him. As he looked around, he realized there was a set of saddlebags beside him. Jesse knew his captors still thought he was unconscious. They also had not started a campfire, so the darkness would help to obscure his movements.

Slowly and carefully sliding himself closer to the saddlebags, Jesse saw the buckle was undone. He lifted the flap and rummaged through the contents. There he found a skinning knife.

Taking the knife, Jesse rolled back over on his side, the way that they had left him. Working slowly, so as to draw no special attention, Jesse began to cut the ropes around his wrists and ankles. He knew the sun would be up in a couple of hours. If he was to help his pa, he knew he must hurry.

***

Joe Clements had been trailing Montana's horse for several hours. Despite the young cowhand's attempts to hide his trail, Joe had been able to stay with it. Squatting on his haunches, Clements studied the signs on the ground, reading them as easily as some men read a newspaper.

The gunfighter saw where Montana's path joined the trail of three others. One of the horses had been ridden by a boy, several hours after the others. He knew those tracks had to belong to Jesse Malone. A dog was walking along with the boy.

The other prints, heading in the same direction, were made by Hinton's mount and a horse ridden by the half Mexican, Julio. He figured them to be a few hours ahead of Jesse. But Joe was worried by what he saw there spelled out before him. Two outlaws were ahead of Jesse and Montana was trailing him. He feared the boy had no idea of the danger he faced.

Walking over to his horse, he removed his canteen. Joe took a long pull of the water and wondered why he ever agreed to take Kimball's tin star. Courtesy had never been a trait he was known for, Clements thought. Gunman or deputy, the jobs were similar. Both professions could get a man killed, the only difference being that his normal jobs paid a lot more for the risks he must take. Joe laughed at the comparison.

Clements knew Malone's son was riding into trouble. For that reason, he continually pushed himself onward. Joe continued tracking them, in spite of the darkness which increasingly made things more difficult. Malone had saved his life once. Clements hoped to return the favor by helping Kell's son.

Joe had been tracking men and animals since he first learned to walk. His skill was well-known, respected as it was feared. Clements had the reputation of a killer—a predator—someone who meticulously stalks his victims the way a huge cat attacks the weak or infirmed. The reputation had not been acquired by accident; Joe was merciless. Once on the trail, he allowed his prey no safety, no place of rest until the victim lost all urge to flee. No one had ever successfully escaped him.

Clements climbed down from his horse and studied the ground, cursing as he did so. It was futile. The darkness made it impossible to follow their tracks any longer. Joe knew it was risky to continue. There was always the chance of marring any existing signs and maybe losing the trail altogether.

Although he found it distasteful, Clements knew he must make camp for the night. On top of everything else, he was worried about the weather and a sudden rain washing out the tracks. After caring for his horse, Joe shook out his bedroll on the ground. There would be no warm fire tonight and no hot coffee to drink. Pulling the blanket up over his shoulders and the hat down over his eyes, Clements knew he was getting close to the outlaws. He closed his eyes. Tomorrow he would take them.

Chapter Twelve

Joe Clements was not the only one who saw Jesse's tracks and knew the boy was headed for an ambush; Kellen Malone saw them too. He knew Jesse was in trouble and he hoped to reach his son before any harm could come to him. Malone knew that time was not on his side, so he made a critical decision.

Kell decided to take another route to the spring. The route he chose was a narrow passageway, which skirted the side of the mountain. The path was little more than a deer trail. The going was faster, but many times more dangerous. Malone had once said it was humanly impossible for a man on horseback. To add to his troubles, the clouds revealed a storm might be on its way.

If Kell succeeded in his attempt, then he could get to Jesse a couple of hours quicker; if he failed, then Kell might never reach Jesse at all! That would leave his son at the mercy of three men who had no mercy to share. But with Jesse needing his help, Malone knew he must try.

The darkness obscured the necessary landmarks and the dim light of the moon offered little relief. After several minutes of searching, Kell finally located the place. Casting a doubtful eye up the trail, he spurred his reluctant horse up the narrow pass.

It was an unlikely way to get to the spring, painstaking and requiring great caution. Sometimes the trail grew so narrow, it became necessary to lead the animal with the stirrups up on top, lashed above the saddle. At all times, they were forced to scramble their way up the precipice, barely suspended between life and death.

Rocks and loose shale littered the pathway, so Kell crept along carefully. Sometimes he was forced to crawl on all fours, feeling his way along the path with his hand. After an hour on the trail, he was several hundred feet above the valley. To stumble was to die.

Then the rains came . . .

The air had grown much cooler, the winds grew stronger, and the danger increased. The brutal rain pelted him fiercely. He pulled out a heavy coat, seeking some of the comfort it offered. He cursed himself for choosing to come this way. It had been a foolhardy decision. Narrow as the path was, there could be no turning back. He was committed. Kell wiped the blowing rain from his eyes, pulled his hat down tighter over his head, and forged ahead.

Just then, a bolt of lightning streaked the sky and Kell could see the path illuminated before him. What path? The sight alone struck fear in the man. If the lightning struck them on the mountainside or the blast hit a tree in their path . . . Kell didn't even want to think about what the outcome might be.

Malone tugged on the reins, the horse trailing along behind. They made their way through another narrow place in the trail, for once the flash of lightning actually helping them in their efforts. Kell breathed a sigh of relief. He started moving again and the wet ground gave way beneath one of his animal's hoofs. The leg slipped out into space and Malone could see him start to slide in the shale.

The horse was thrashing wildly. Kell pulled harder on the lead reins. "Come on, horse! Fight!" he yelled, the voice drowned out in the deafening thunderclaps.

Malone locked his heels in the mud, but felt himself sliding also. Sweat poured from his body and his muscles burned like fire. Wisdom told him he should turn loose of the reins or they both might perish. But Kell could not bring himself to give into the urges.

"Don't give up!" he shouted furiously. "Doggone it! Don't give up!"

His mount continued to slide, the weight of the animal pulling Kell to the ground. One moment he was praying; then Malone let loose a string of profanities that would have made a harlot blush. Sliding on his chest and elbows, but still clinging to the reins, Kell was pulled closer to certain death.

The frightened animal seemed to sense that Malone was trying to save him. Kell could see a fire in his eyes, as it struggled to regain its footing. The horse scrambled up over the ledge, shaking his head and blowing his nostrils in triumph. Malone came to his feet, brushing the mud and shale from his chest. He patted the horse on the neck. "That was close, boy. Too close!"

After their brush with death, Malone continued ahead, directed more by sense than by sight. Kell checked his watch during one of the lightning flashes. It would be light soon.

The air was thinner at this altitude and he stopped more often to catch his breath. Kell tried not to look down. Oftentimes the horse balked, unwilling to continue. Somehow, Malone always managed to urge him onward.

Kell finally let out a sigh of relief. He was almost there . . .

***

Because of the incessant rain and the miserable conditions, the outlaws were starting to grow weary and impatient. They had not eaten in hours, there was no warm coffee, and they were not dressed for the weather.

"I tell you, Montana, he's not coming," Deke grumbled bitterly, pulling the blanket tighter around him. "I'm getting tired of waiting. Besides, I need to see a doctor. Let's just kill the kid and get it over with."

Hodges was insistent. "Malone will be here, Deke. You just shut your mouth and wait!"

Montana looked over at the boy and saw he'd heard Hinton's remark. He did not see the knife the boy had or the ropes that were now loose from the young man's hands and feet.

Sadly, Montana knew Hinton was right about one thing. Sooner or later, they would have to kill Jesse. He wondered how he had ever gotten into this mess. The cowhand hung his head in shame.

Jesse had freed his hands from the ropes several minutes ago, but he was still unsure what his next move should be. The ropes were still visible around his wrists and ankles, but they did nothing to restrain him. Cold and wet from the bitter downpour, Jesse shivered and waited for an opening.

***

As Kell made his way closer, he could hear the men talking near his campsite. He was sure one of the voices belonged to Montana. He tied his horse to a tree and sat down on a stump to check his guns.

The rain was finally stopped, with only an occasional lightning flash to brighten the cloud-filled, early morning sky. Kell shook the rain from his hat and removed his wet, bulky coat, so nothing would restrict his movements.

As he sat there, something nudged Kell in ribs. He turned with a start. There was Lobo sitting beside him. The dog was licking at the wound on his hind leg.

"What happened to you, boy?" Kell whispered, gently petting the animal "Nice to finally see a friendly face."

Malone removed his neckerchief and carefully bandaged the dog's leg. "There, that ought to hold you. You hang tight now, Lobo. When I come back, I'll have Jesse with me."

Kell took a deep breath, drew his guns, and stole a look between the rocks. Just then, a shot rang out from inside the camp . . .

***

Finally, Deke Hinton had waited long enough. Not waiting for Montana's approval, he threw aside the blanket and palmed his gun.

"I've said it before. The man isn't coming! And if you don't have the gumption to do what needs to be done, Hodges, then I'll do it myself."

He walked back towards Jesse and grabbed him by the shirt collar, jerking the boy to his feet. As he pulled him up, the ropes fell from the boy's wrists and ankles.

"What the . . .!" he grunted, as Jesse viciously slashed at the man with his knife.

The boy did no real damage, but cut through Deke's shirt and left a bloody stripe across the man's chest. Hinton cursed the boy and leveled his gun to shoot him. The shot hit nothing as Jesse scrambled back into the rocks.

As Deke started to give chase, two quick shots sounded from the darkness. One of the shots knocked the hat from Hinton's head. The other shot staggered Julio, as a bullet punctured the fleshy part of his left shoulder.

"Run, Jesse!" A voice shouted. "Run!"

"That has to be Malone!" Hodges grumbled, taking cover behind a rock. "He came up the mountain behind us."

Deke was skeptical. "You're crazy! He must have been up here waiting for us. Ain't no man could come up the mountain that way! Nothing human . . . not in this storm."

Julio nodded in agreement, as Montana tried to bandage the Mexican's shoulder.

"Don't you underestimate Kellen Malone!" Montana warned. "I've known him for a long time and nothing he does surprises me. You may not like him, Deke, but don't you low-rate him. Kell won't back down from nothing!"

"Diablo hombre!" Julio muttered in disbelief.

Troubled by this latest revelation, Hinton was feeling belligerent. "Listen, Breed! I've heard just about enough of this Mex talk! Why don't you try speaking English for a change? Diablo hombre . . . what's that mean anyway?"

Weary of Hinton's insults and fearful of the man on the mountain with them, the Mexican's dark eyes turned cold. He stared at Hinton for several seconds before he spoke. "It means devil man."

Julio had always believed in demons and the supernatural. A man riding straight up the side of a mountain—he knew it wasn't humanly possible. Not a man! And now they were trying to kill the devil man's son. The Mexican suddenly wished he were far away from this place.

The sisters at the mission tried to steer him down the right paths when he was a little boy. He often wondered why he failed to listen to them. Then Julio recalled the premonition that came to him earlier that day, an ominous vision that foretold his death. He breathed a prayer and quickly crossed himself.

After Montana finished bandaging Julio's shoulder, he pulled his six-gun from the holster and checked the cylinders. Satisfied, he holstered the gun.

"Deke, if I didn't need your help finding the boy," Montana blustered, "then I would kill you right now! You and Julio get out there and find them! Now! If we don't kill them, then it is the gallows for all of us."

***

When Jesse sprang back into the darkness, he was startled by the pair of gunshots that were fired only a few feet from where he had been. He wasn't absolutely certain who had done the shooting, but he knew he must find somewhere safe to hide.

His mysterious protector had called him by name, so the boy thought it might be his father. Jesse's hopes were lifted by the idea. Yet he knew if the man in the dark was Kellen Malone, then he had already done the impossible, scaling the backside of the mountain in the storm. And if it was his pa, he would also know to look for Jesse at the cave.

Then he remembered that his mother had once told him that his father would gladly risk his life to protect the two of them. Since the statement was made after his father went to prison, Jesse had foolishly chosen not to believe her. The events of this day made him believe he had been wrong.

Twice that night, Kellen Malone had risked his life to save the boy, once by scaling the mountain and the other by confronting his captors. Jesse dearly hoped the two of them lived through the night! He had so many things to say to his father.

Moving quickly, Jesse sensed someone was behind him. The boy regretted that he had dropped the knife during his escape from Hinton. Jesse raced towards the entrance of the cave. If he still remembered the way, the cave should be just ahead.

As he scrambled inside the small opening, a familiar voice spoke, "Good to see you again, Jesse. I suppose you forgot about telling me about this secret place you and your pa shared."

While using a couple of words his mother would have washed out his mouth for uttering, Jesse stared into the eyes of Montana Hodges ...

***

After firing at the outlaws, Kell's first priority was finding his son. As much as he desired to kill these men, Kell knew he must make sure his son was safe. Malone made his way towards the cave, figuring it had to be the most likely place the boy would go.

Already exhausted from the climb up the mountain, Malone summoned every ounce of energy he had left. Guns drawn, Kell ran towards the cave, where he had cached the extra ammunition. Before this was over, Malone figured he might need it to kill the men who had tried to harm Jesse.

Kell was thirty feet away from the cave's entrance when he saw Julio just ahead of him in the darkness. Creeping up behind the Mexican, he shoved both six-guns against the man's lower back.

"Drop the guns, Julio, or I'll kill you!"

"No, Kell," Montana said. "You drop your guns or I'll kill the boy!"

A sick feeling came to Kell's stomach when he saw Montana with his arm around Jesse's neck and a gun pressed to the boy's head. Just then, Deke Hinton also emerged from the darkness, with his gun leveled towards Kell.

Under normal circumstances, Malone might have tried to take the three of them in a gunfight. But he knew that Jesse would probably be killed in the crossfire. Although it pained him to do it, Kell reluctantly dropped his guns.

"Guess I shouldn't have told Montana about the cave," Jesse said. "Sorry, Pa. And I want you to know I'm sorry about a whole lot of things."

"Don't worry about it, kid. It'll be all right."

"Don't you count on it, Malone," Hinton gloated. "You two won't live to see another sunset."

A flash of lightning revealed Hinton's torn clothes and the bite marks Lobo had inflicted on the man. "What happened to you, Deke? Maybe that's why the dog looked like he ate something that didn't agree with him."

Viciously, Hinton slammed Kell across the skull with his rifle butt. Malone was knocked to the ground, stunned but conscious. As Jesse quickly knelt beside his father, Kell merely smiled at the man who had hit him.

"Leave them alone!" Montana ordered. "There'll be time for that later."

"Thanks for coming to help me, Pa."

"Fine job I did of it!" Kell grumbled. "But you handled yourself pretty good back there, Jesse. It made me proud."

"Thanks, Pa."

"Tell me, Montana," he said, looking up at Hodges. "What's a friend's life sell for these days?"

"I've heard just about enough of this!" Hinton said, still sore about Malone's killing of his brother, Sam. "Let's just plug 'em, Montana! Get it over with.

"Just hold on, Deke! I'm still running things here." Hodges squatted down on his haunches beside them. "I didn't do it for the money, Kell . . . not at first. You've got to believe that. There's a whole lot more to it."

"I know all about you and the Hinton boys robbing the stage. Still don't have a clue why you did it."

"Clay just wanted your ranch. Told him you'd never sell it. So he came up with a plan to get you out of the way."

Both of the other men had guns trained on them. Malone could see they were growing impatient with the conversation. He wondered how much longer Montana could hold them off.

"I figured that much. But it still doesn't explain your part in this, Montana."

"You can blame Alice for that."

"He tried to steal your wife!" Jesse exploded.

"Yea, I guess you're right, son. I spent a lot of time at the ranch with you, Kell. Alice was always there, looking so young and pretty. You know how she was, smiling and friendly to everyone," Montana explained. "Guess I got kind of taken with her . . . couldn't get her off my mind. Even fooled myself into believing she felt the same way about me."

As Malone listened to the story, the anger boiled over inside him. He watched for an opening, some way to save their lives and to kill these men.

"As long as I draw a breath, Montana, you'd better never stop riding. Don't ever quit watching over your shoulder, because I'm coming to kill you!"

"Guess I'd feel the same way if I was you. I knew Adkins wanted your ranch and I wanted you out of the way. One thing just led to another . . . so we figured to smooth out two broncs with one saddle. Carlton Stadler, he came along later."

Looking over at Jesse, Kell could see the hurt in his eyes. Along with the fact his son had lost his mother, the boy also felt betrayed by his friend.

"I spent so much time at your house," Montana continued, "it was easy to pick up your pocket watch. Well, you know what happened from there."

"What about Alice? Why did she have to die?"

"That was an accident, Kell . . . I swear it! With you out of the pic-ture, I thought she'd begin to care about me. Boy, was I wrong! Alice never loved anyone but you." Montana removed his hat and ran his fingers through his hair. Then he returned it to his head. "One day I tried to force my attentions on her and things got a little out of hand. We struggled and she fell against a rock. I told everyone a horse kicked her."

Malone could see a tear in his son's eye. The only emotion he could feel right now was hatred for the man who had once been his friend.

"I felt guilty for Jesse's loss, Kell. I tried to be a friend to him in your absence." He looked over at Jesse. "I hope you understand that I'm real sorry."

Jesse spat in his face.

"Reckon I deserved that," Montana said, wiping his face with his neckerchief. Then he started towards his horse

"What about selling whiskey to the Chiricahuas, Montana?" Kell asked, stopping Hodges in mid-stride. "How did you get involved in that?"

"That was all Stadler's doing. Adkins had nothing to do with it. I'd love to tell you more, but I have to be on my way." Hodges swung himself into the saddle.

Kell sneered at the man. "Guess you don't have the stomach to finish your own killing."

Montana ignored the comment, looking down at the two other outlaws. "Deke, you and Julio, give me a couple of minutes to get on down the trail. Then you take care of things here."

Hinton grinned wickedly. "It'll be my pleasure . . . and I do mean a pleasure!"

Julio said nothing as he stood next to the horses. He was already having second thoughts about the murder of a boy. Still, he kept his gun trained on Kellen Malone.

Montana reined his horse around. "Sorry, boys. Wish things could have been different."

Jesse and Kell said nothing as they watched him gallop away.

Chapter Thirteen

While Hinton and Julio maintained an eye on his prisoners, Deke kept checking his watch like a man who was late for an appointment. The rains had fully stopped and lightning bolts streaked the sky in the distance. A bank of clouds still overpowered the morning sun, but they would soon yield themselves to the beginning of a bright new day.

Checking the sky, Kell could see the clouds were quickly breaking up and it was roughly thirty minutes until daylight. He knew nothing but darkness awaited them if he failed to act.

"So, Malone, how do you want to die?" Hinton said.

"How about giving me both my guns back, Deke, and you can kill me any time you're good and ready?"

Hinton booted Malone in the ribs with his boot. "You think you're pretty funny, don't you, Malone? We'll see how much you're laughing in hell."

"Then why don't you get it over with, Hinton? I'd rather be dead than have to listen to any more of your mouth!"

"Now it's my turn," Hinton said with a grin. "You killed my brother, Malone. Now I'm gonna make you watch your son die," he snarled, turning the gun on Jesse.

"No!" Malone screamed, springing from the ground and bulling into Hinton with his shoulder. The gun fell from Deke's hand and Kell grabbed for it.

At the same time, the Mexican wheeled around to face the man who had tackled Hinton. The lightning flashed as his gun came level . . .

For one split second, Julio saw the bitter face of Kellen Malone, illuminated like a specter of death. In his hand was a six-gun and its muzzle blossomed flame. Kell squeezed the trigger twice and both bullets found their mark.

The big slugs staggered the Mexican and he fell over backwards in a heap. The gun tumbled from his weakening hand. Julio tried to speak to the sister at the mission, whose face he saw in the clouds. Then the words failed to come and his eyes saw nothing at all.

Deke came to his feet and ran for cover, looking for a Winchester. Malone snapped a quick shot at him and missed. Jesse scooped up Kell's guns and headed for the cave. Malone was scarcely a step behind him.

"Come on boy! Let's get inside now!"

Jesse clawed his way inside the cave as Kell pushed him through the opening. Malone turned quickly to cover their back. He snapped a quick shot at Deke, who fired as he gave chase. As bullets kicked dust and fragments all around him, Kell dived inside. A bullet split the air where his body had just been.

"Whew! That was close," Jesse said.

"Yes, it was."

"Pa, Montana killed Clay. He shot Sheriff Kimball too."

"Yeah, I know it. Rachel told me before I came looking for you."

From the mouth of the cave, Kell fired two quick shots at Hinton, who ducked behind the rocks for cover. His return fire kicked fragments in Kell's face.

"Miss Rachel cares about you . . . she told me so."

"I know that too," he said, watching for a clean shot at Hinton.

A wry look came to the boy's face. "Since the two of you are on a first name basis, the feeling must go both ways."

Kell smiled. "How did you ever get to be so nosy?"

For several minutes, Deke and Kell traded gunfire. Then the shooting stopped for a time. Knowing Hinton had not gone anywhere, Kell immediately grew suspicious.

"He's up to something, Jesse. I can feel it."

They had only a short time wait.

"Malone!" he yelled. "Kellen Malone!" After making his way back to his horse and removing something from his saddlebag, Hinton had crept around to the side of the cave. From there, Kell had no way to see him without exposing himself to gunfire.

"What do you want, Deke?"

"You and your boy like it in that cave so much, I'm gonna make sure you two stay there forever." Malone heard the outlaw laughing. "I've got a stick of dynamite out here. That cave will make a right, fine tomb for you."

"You're bluffing, Deke. If you had some dynamite, you'd have used it already."

Kell did his best to see outside without catching a bullet. The outlaw's threat had him worried, not just for his own life, but also for that of his son.

"I'm not bluffing. I just wanted you to know what was coming. "Goodbye, Malone!"

Risky as it was, Kell crawled forward and chanced a look around the mouth of the cave. What he saw sent a chill though him.

A lighted stick of dynamite came hurtling through the air, towards the cave's entrance.

Malone knew there would be no chance to throw the stick away, once outside the cave's shelter. Hinton would delight in shooting him down the very second he appeared in the open. Kell swallowed hard. It looked like the end for both of them.

Covering his son's body, Kell was helpless to do anything but watch . . .

***

The shrill cracks of gunfire echoed from off the mountaintop, breaking the reverent stillness of a fresh, new morning.

Montana Hodges breathed a sigh of relief, glad the deed was finally finished. The young cowhand could find no rejoicing in his victory. His actions had led to the death of some good people, including a fine, young boy. With them dead, Montana thought, maybe he could put the past behind him.

He urged his horse along the gently winding trail, glad that he hadn't been a witness to the boy's death. Kellen Malone said that Montana had changed. This he knew and accepted.

Hodges began to think about what he would do now. He was certain that nothing could ever be the same. No longer could he return to Redhawk, after gunning down the sheriff. He decided to just start riding west and see just where the trail would take him. A change of scenery might keep the old ghosts from returning to his mind. Montana knew he must give it a try.

Once there, Montana could build a whole new life with the large sum of money that Stadler had paid him. Gone were the cheap barmaids! No longer a struggling cowhand, he figured a better class of woman might be attracted to him now. Perhaps he would find a woman devoted to him only—someone like Alice Malone.

He drew rein in front of a rippling creek, a stream that would be as dry as powder in another week. Allowing his horse a chance to drink, Montana climbed down to fill his canteen. The young cowhand sank his face down in the water, drinking long and deep. Then something grabbed his attention . . .

The gunfire continued.

Montana knew this wasn't a good sign. Something must have gone wrong. A couple of shots he might have expected, maybe three or four.

This was too many! Panic and uncertainty gripped his mind. What had happened?

He swore loudly. It could only mean one thing . . . Kellen Malone was still alive.

In such a hurry that he forgot about his canteen, Hodges ran to his horse. Momentarily unsure of what to do, he forked the saddle and reined the horse towards the mountaintop.

If Kell got away, Montana knew Carlton Stadler would surely kill him. In addition, Jesse's testimony could send him to the gallows. But worst of all, each of these fates would have to wait in line behind the terrible wrath of Kellen Malone! Montana had seen exhibitions of his rage before. And with Malone alive, there was no place in the world where he might be safe!

None of these options particularly appealed to him.

Montana's only chance at life was linked to the death of his friend. The choice was not a difficult one to make. He would have to kill Malone and the boy himself! It was something he should have done in the first place, instead of trusting the task to Deke Hinton and the Mexican. He cussed himself for being foolish enough to think the pair of them might be capable of besting the man.

Brutally jamming the spurs to his mount, the frightened, young cowhand galloped up the mountainside.

Suddenly, the mountain reverberated with a loud explosion. Montana's horse, startled by the blast, reared high into the air. The rider struggled to stay in the saddle and the horse bucked wildly. No longer able to hold on, Hodges was thrown to the ground and dashed his head against a rock.

He tried to stand to his feet, but couldn't. Montana's world became a place of confused shapes and visions, before it went totally dark . . .

***

As Kell saw the dynamite come flying through the air, he sadly realized he could do nothing. Expecting the worst, Malone threw his body on top of Jesse, hoping to shield him from the blast.

Certain that it would be his last, Malone stole another look out the mouth of cave. To his astonishment, he saw the wounded dog running in their direction.

The stick of dynamite landed on the ground, five feet in front of the entrance to the cave. Lobo quickly caught it up in his teeth. The animal went running up into the rocks—playing the game as he had been taught—retrieving the stick for its thrower.

Deke Hinton could not believe what he was seeing. The dog was headed his way with the lighted stick of dynamite. Fearing for his own life, Deke ran towards his horse. Lobo thought it was part of the game. The faster Hinton ran, the more determined the dog became to catch him.

The outlaw, frantic to get away, was no match for the speed of the dog. Just when he thought he might successfully escape, Hinton stumbled on a rock. His tail wagging, Lobo offered the stick to him, its fuse nearly gone . . .

The dynamite exploded with a deafening roar, as if it shook the entire mountainside. Fire flew into the air, as the blast sent rocks, dirt, and remains showering all around them.

Still covering Jesse, Kell stayed there on the ground for several minutes, until things calmed around them. As quickly as it had taken place, the world was strangely silent. His mind would not accept what he had just seen happen. A kind, black dog gave his life while saving theirs, all because of a simple game he learned as a pup.

"What happened, Pa?" asked Jesse, his eyes still wide with fear.

"Deke threw a stick of dynamite our way, son. Lobo thought it was a game and carried it back to him. He's gone, Jesse."

No further explanations were necessary as Kell crawled out into the sunshine. Jesse followed close behind him.

Realization, then sadness were showing in the boy's face. "Lobo was a good dog, Pa."

"That he was, son."

Finding a shovel among Julio's belonging, Kell and Jesse dug a couple of graves. One of them was for the Mexican. The other was for what was left of Deke Hinton, little though it was. After tamping in the handmade crosses, Kell removed his hat and spoke a few words over them. As hard as he tried, there wasn't much of anything good to say about the pair, except for the fact that they were gone from this earth.

Jesse looked at his father. "Let's go home, pa."

Kell nodded. The words had a nice ring to them.

Spooked as the animals were from the blast, it took them some time to catch their horses. Kell and Jesse tightened up the cinches and loaded up the extra guns. Then they started down the trail for home. But Jesse was oddly quiet as they rode.

"What's eating at you, son? Is it the dog?"

"Not really." The boy hung his head. "Maybe a little, I guess. Mostly I wondered about Montana, Pa. What do you plan to do about him?"

"I'm going to kill him, Jesse!" Malone said, rage filling his soul. "I know it sounds hard to you. But the man killed your mother and cost me seven years of my life. Worst of all, he nearly took my son away from me too! Montana's got to pay for what he's done. I plan to make sure he does!"

"And Carlton Stadler?"

"Before this day ends, I'll see both of them dead!"

At that moment, gunfire broke out below them . . .

***

After several minutes, Montana came to his senses, his head throbbing in pain. Like a bad dream, he vaguely remembered being thrown from his horse. As he sat there in the dust, shaking his head to clear away the dizziness, he recalled the events leading up to the explosion.

The young cowhand came to his feet slowly, still wobbly from the blow to the skull. Looking all around him, he could see his horse nowhere. Montana began walking in the direction the animal had run.

A couple of hundred yards later, he could see a rider coming up the trail. Hodges squinted into the sunlight. He smiled as he saw the rider was leading another horse.

He recognized the man to be Joe Clements.

Clements pulled back on the reins, stopping his horse. "Lose something, Montana?"

"Yeah," he said, walking over to take hold of the reins. "Thanks for finding him for me, Skull." Hodges stared at Clements curiously. "What are you doing way up here?"

"I was looking for you, Montana." Clements pulled back his vest to reveal a badge. "I lost your tracks in the storm."

"Redhawk must be getting desperate for lawmen."

"Same thing I told 'em. Now, where's Malone?"

"Still up on the mountaintop, Skull."

"And the boy?"

"He's up there too. They were both in good shape the last time I saw them."

Clements' eyes were still and humorless. "You're under arrest, Hodges."

Montana laughed, thinking the statement was a joke.

"I'm not pulling your leg, Montana! I'm placing you under arrest."

The humor in his eyes gave way to a cold, bitter glare. "How do you figure to do it, Skull?"

"I don't care how I take you in. Alive or dead . . . makes no difference to me. It all pays the same." Clements deliberately built a smoke as he talked. "Arresting you is my job, but it's also a personal thing with me.

"I don't have much use for a man who betrays his friends. A man like that just ain't fit for wasting good air." He shoved the cigarette between his lips, striking a match on the saddle. Joe lit the end, pulling deeply as it started to glow. "One way or the other, I'm taking you in. It's your choice, Hodges. You can ride tall in the saddle or be tied across it."

"I'm not going anywhere with you, Skull . . . not as a prisoner! What kind of fair trial could I get? No, I don't think so. You go on back to town and leave me to go about my business."

Clements hard face showed no expression. "I can't do it, Montana. That train's already left the station."

"Then you'll have to go for your gun. Besides, I think you're overrated anyway."

"It'll cost you lead to find out. This ain't no horse race, Montana. No ribbons are given to second place . . . the loser dies!"

"That's the way it will have to be then."

Montana was still smiling as his hand swept down for his gun . . .

The young cowhand's six-gun cleared leather in the sound of a heartbeat, probably his fastest draw ever. Triumph showed in his eyes. He had beaten the legendary Skull Clements.

But Joe was already firing.

A pair of slugs stained Montana's shirt as his gun found a target. Joe triggered his gun again, this shot hitting not two inches away from the other two. The young man's lifeless body fell from his saddle and hit the ground, without ever getting off a single shot.

As Joe holstered his gun, he quietly cursed the dead young man. For the first time in years, it was a killing he didn't want.

Chapter Fourteen

As their horses charged down off the mountain, Kell saw a man tying a body over the saddle. He was still too far away to recognize the man. But he did recognize the pair of horses.

The one with the body across the saddle belonged to Montana.

"Howdy, Joe" Kell said, drawing rein next to the body. "Looks like you saved me a bullet."

Fully aware of their presence, Clements never stopped to look up until he was done with the task at hand.

"Or the town the cost of a hanging," Joe added. Clements shook his head in frustration. "What a waste, Kell! There was no good reason for him to die like that. It's like he wanted it to happen."

"You might be right," Kell replied. "Maybe he did."

As Jesse stared at the dead body of his friend, he felt a little sick to his stomach. Then he hung his head. Although Montana had tried to kill him, he felt no hatred towards the man, only remorse over his death.

Clements, who always had a weakness for kids, looked over at Jesse and smiled. "Who's this good looking fellow there with you, Malone?"

"This is my son Jesse." Then he pointed at the scar-faced gunman. "Jesse, this is Joe Clements, a good friend of mine."

"Better than this one, I hope," he said, nodding at Montana's body. Joe reached out to shake the boy's hand. "Hey! You've got a strong handshake, kid. I like that in a young man." He could see the boy swelled with pride at the compliment. "You've got a good man for a pa."

Jesse smiled, looking over at his father. "I know it, sir. Well, at least I do now."

"What are you going to do now, Malone?"

"I'm going after Stadler, but first I have to look in on Rachel."

"I know it ain't none of my business, but you'd be a fool to let that one get away from you," Joe offered. "Women are scarce in this country, the good ones even scarcer!"

"You're right about that," Kell replied. "How's Bill doing?"

"The old sawbones seems to think he'll make it. Kimball asked me to take over until he's up and around." He polished the star with his sleeve. "I'm not used to being on this side of the badge. Not sure yet whether I like it or not. But I do gotta admit, it kind of grows on a man . . . not looking over your shoulder for a posse.

"This thing with Stadler is something for the law to handle. It's my job to arrest him. You understand that, don't you, Malone? Now I'll get to it in a few hours . . . just you wait. I've got to take care of this body first," he said with a wink. "You try to avoid him until then. But if you do happen to run into Stadler, just tell him he's under arrest. If that don't work, then I reckon you wouldn't have any choice but to kill him. The eyes of justice will look the other way, if you know what I mean."

"Thanks, Joe."

"Think nothing of it. I owe you, Malone." His face turned serious. "You be careful. Stadler's a shootist . . . I'm sure of it! His name's still lost to me, but I'll come up with it."

"Something about the man is familiar to me too," he replied. "Maybe I arrested him one time, back when I was keeping the peace in Kansas."

"Wait a minute, Malone! Did you say Kansas?" His eyes grew wide with recognition. "Now I know! You remember the blond fellow who called you a liar in the saloon? Well, that was Yance Candrey. I knew something about Stadler rang a bell."

"Yeah," Kell observed. "There's a strong resemblance."

"I'll lay money on it, Malone. Carlton Stadler is Yance's cousin, Tom Candrey."

"I think you've got something there. Not too many folks know what Tom looks like, but the two of them usually wind up in the same places."

"You mark my words! He'll never let anybody take him alive . . . not Tom Candrey." Joe climbed back into the saddle. "I'll take Montana's body back to town. Every man deserves a decent burial, even dirty, low-down scum who turn on their friends. Good luck to you, Malone."

"You too, Joe."

Clements tipped his hat to the boy. "Jesse, you be sure and take care of your pa now. The man can't keep himself out of trouble."

Jesse smiled. "I'll do my best."

Clements waved to them as he started back the trail to Redhawk.

***

Nervously, Rachel paced back and forth on the steps of the verandah. She stopped occasionally to stare at the horizon and then resumed her walking.

Denton Turner often found women mildly interesting. Although he liked the way they looked and smelled, the species always left him feeling uncomfortable. It was one of the reasons he joined the army in the first place, to be away from them. He now found himself a nursemaid to one of the more attractive of their species. Annoyed by the woman's constant pacing, Denton was beginning to grow restless himself.

Turner now regretted the fact that he had let Buck Halstead go back to town to resume his barkeeping duties. Despite the fact it was necessary for someone to remain here to protect the woman, Turner wished he had gone with Buck.

"I wish you would sit down, Miss Payton," the sergeant replied, removing his hat.

Manners had never been something he fully understood. He started to put the hat back on, but should he? Then he wondered what to do with his hands. Suddenly, Denton wished he was back in the desert chasing Geronimo.

"How can I relax, Mr. Turner? I'm worried about them."

"Don't you worry about Kellen Malone. The man can certainly take care of himself." He did his best to force a smile. "If anyone can find the boy, it'll be him, ma'am."

Rachel stared at the young man. "You act as though you know him, Mr. Turner. How long have you been friends?"

Denton smiled politely, wondering if he should tip his hat each time he spoke. "I just met him, ma'am. But you can trust me . . . I know the type."

"How is that?"

Turner pondered over the question, wondering how much he should dare reveal. Yet he would do anything if it would cease the woman's pacing.

"Ma'am, I am Sergeant Denton Turner with the United States Army."

"But you look so young!" she replied in astonishment. "Does Kell know this?"

"Yes, he does, Miss Payton. I asked him to remain quiet as to my identity." Turner continued his explanation. "I am a soldier, ma'am. That being the case, I know many men like Kellen Malone. And of him, I know much."

"You do, sergeant? Please tell me about him."

"Your Kellen Malone fought in the War Between the States, Miss Payton. At that time, he was little more than a boy himself. He served under General Custer. His bravery under fire was rewarded numerous times. The man is a legend."

"I had no idea," she said. Rachel resumed her pacing, stopping only to stare at the mountain. "Sergeant, what was that book you were thumbing through earlier? The one you got out of Clay's belongings."

Turner increasingly grew more perplexed. He felt the information should remain confidential, but he was uncomfortable telling the woman it was none of her business. "Women!" he muttered, just under his breath. "Why would anybody want one?"

"What did you say, sergeant? I couldn't hear you.

"Nothing, ma'am," Turner replied, his face turning several shades of red. He squeezed the battered, leather-bound book in his hand. "It's a ledger, Miss Payton. The information in it will help to clear Mr. Malone." Denton knew he had already said too much.

Rachel could scarcely believe what she heard. "It will clear his name? How?"

Now I've gone and done it, Denton thought. He wondered how he might talk his way out of this one. Talking—that was the thing which caused his problem in the first place!

Suddenly, Rachel leaped from the verandah, running down the steps. Turner then saw the reason for her reaction. A pair of riders was coming towards them. Never in his life had he been so happy for an interruption!

As Kell and Jesse got down from their horses, Rachel didn't know which one to hug first. She embraced each of them several times.

"I'm so glad you're both safe." She saw the dog missing. "Where's Lobo?"

Jesse hung his head.

Kell spoke up first. "We've got a lot of things to tell you, Rachel, but they'll have to wait." As he checked his guns, he said. "Turner and I have some business in town first." Kell nodded at the sergeant. "Thanks for protecting Miss Payton."

Turner walked down the steps, still carrying the ledger. He handed the book to Kell. "You'd better read this, Malone."

Kell quickly thumbed through a couple of pages, scanning them with a cocked eyebrow. He looked up at the sergeant. "Adkins liked to keep track of everything, didn't he?"

"That he did, sir."

"So Clay *wasn't* responsible for the trading with the Chiricahuas! That confirms what Montana told me. Stadler was working behind the scenes the whole time."

"Yes," Turner replied. "Adkins probably figured this book was his insurance against a double-cross. Lucky thing he never got around to telling Stadler about it—or Tom Candrey, whatever his name is."

Malone looked up from the book. "What are we waiting for, Denton?" He tossed the ledger to Turner. "Let's go get him!"

Turner shook his head. "It's too late, Malone. Tom Candrey and his cousin, Yance, are already gone."

"Gone?"

"Yes, they fled town. After I found the book, I wired ahead for some troops. They were here in a matter of hours. But by the time they arrived, it was too late." Turner swelled with pride at his next revelation. "At least it wasn't a total loss. They'll be able to place Skull Clements in shackles."

"Arrest Clements? Why? He's the only law left in Redhawk."

"Not anymore he isn't," Denton muttered. "The troops will stay until the sheriff is back on his feet or a U.S. Marshal arrives, whichever comes first."

Rachel interrupted. "But that's martial law."

"Yes, Dent. You can't do that!" added Malone.

The sergeant stood as tall as his frame would allow, only about three inches over five feet. "The United States Army can do whatever it pleases," he declared defiantly. Then growing ashamed of his tone, Dent added, "There's nothing anyone can do about it now. Skull Clements is a criminal."

Malone was puzzled. "Well, what did they arrest him for, Dent?"

Turner flipped his way through the book, stopping as soon as he saw the right page. Then he pointed at a paragraph in the ledger. "You see right here" he asked, pointing towards an entry in Clay's own handwriting. "Ten years ago, Adkins paid Skull Clements to kill Jace Cline. Now I'll grant you, Jace was a murdering cutthroat, but no one has the right to kill another man."

"But I heard Cline drew first."

"That may well be true, but with a man like Skull Clements, it was still murder, pure and simple! Now I have all the proof I need. I ordered him placed under arrest, immediately upon his return."

"Let me see that again," Malone said, turning the book as if to read it easier. While Turner smugly watched, Kell quickly ripped the page from the ledger.

The sergeant couldn't believe his eyes. "What are you doing, Malone? That book is the property of the United States government. You can't do that!"

"Just watch me!" Malone pulled a match from his pocket, striking it on the side of his boot. Denton tried to stop him, but Kell simply elbowed the smaller man away. Malone lit the piece of paper, holding it aloft as it burned. "Well," he said with a smile, "there goes all your proof." It fell to the ground, charred beyond recognition.

Rachel and Jesse burst out in laughter.

Sergeant Turner was beside himself. Part of his anger was caused by Malone destroying the evidence. The other could be blamed on embarrassment, having just been humiliated in front of a woman and a boy.

"I'll have you jailed for that!"

"So what else is new? You saw the book, Dent. I just spent seven years paying for something I didn't do." Smugly, Malone glared at the sergeant. "At least this time I'll be guilty of something."

Kell liked the young sergeant and hoped to reason with him. "Look at this way, Dent. Joe Clements hasn't always been a model citizen, I'll give you that. But the man is trying to live on the right side of the law. Why don't you give him a chance?"

"But justice has to be served!"

Staying silent no longer, Rachel proceeded to gang up on him. "What's the justice in a good man going to jail? Cline drew first."

"Look, Dent. I just paid for something I didn't do." He smiled at the soldier. "And Joe is going to go free for something he did. It's a fair trade. Some might even call it redemption."

"You just can't barter justice, Malone."

"What choice do you have? There is no evidence."

Turner was not willing to give this up so easily. "Miss Payton saw you!" he shouted. "She can testify to it."

Suddenly, Rachel looked confused. "Saw what, Sergeant Turner?"

"You two are in this thing together! But the boy saw you!"

Jesse smiled. "Guess I didn't see anything either, sir."

The sergeant threw up his hands in frustration. "I guess I have no choice but to have Clements released," Turner said belligerently. Gracious in defeat, he was not.

Kell walked between Rachel and Jesse, draping his arms around their shoulders. He led the two of them up the stairs towards the front door. "I hope you have something to eat in there, Rachel," he said with a smile. "Jesse and I are hungry."

"Sergeant, are you hungry?" Rachel asked. "You care to join us?"

Turner nodded, mumbling something about women and others of their species as he followed them inside.

***

After just finishing his breakfast at the diner, Malone walked down the street, whistling a tune. He made his way over to the sheriff's office, pushing open the door without knocking.

"How are you doing, Joe?" he asked.

"It's good to see you, Malone," Clements said, his feet resting on the desk. "Where you been keeping yourself? Never mind! I can tell just by looking. Been spending a lot of time with Miss Payton, I see."

Malone just nodded with a smile.

"Kimball should be up and around," Joe said, "in another two or three weeks!"

"That's good to hear!" Malone added.

"Yeah, it is. Been getting the urge to wander a little. Job's a little too reputable for me."

The two of them shared a laugh.

"You hear anything of Tom Candrey?"

"Yeah," Joe replied. "They said he killed a man over in Denver, couple of weeks ago. At least he's nowhere around here."

The twinkle in his eyes quickly disappeared. "It isn't over, Joe. I think you know that, don't you?"

Clements nodded. "Yea, I think you're right. I've had a bad feeling about this for some time now." Joe's mind drifted to another topic. "I talked to Sergeant Turner, Malone. You probably know the man doesn't like me much! I want to thank you for what you did for me. Heard all about it from Jesse."

"Aw, it was nothing!"

"You should be proud of that boy, Malone. Make a good man someday!"

"I know it."

Just then, the door burst open, Breathless from his news, Jesse came running inside. "Sorry I didn't knock, Mr. Clements!"

"That's okay, kid. What can I do for you?"

"Did you two hear the news?" His eyes bubbled over with excitement. "Geronimo surrendered today in Skeleton Canyon! Buck told me."

Malone hung his head.

"What's the matter, Pa?

"I just hate to hear about anyone giving up his freedom, son. I know a little bit about that." He tousled the boy's hair. "Don't you forget, Jesse. You're part Indian yourself."

"I knew it was bound to happen," Joe muttered. "Nelson Miles is like a hungry dog with a piece of meat. He just won't let go!"

"Come on, Jesse." Malone got up to leave. "We ought to tell Rachel." The two of them started through the door.

Clements called after them. "See you later, boys."

When Kell and Jesse arrived at the diner, they noticed the doors were locked and the shades were pulled down. "I was just here," Kell grumbled. "They couldn't be closed."

All at once, a chill crept up his spine. Kell refused to believe what he was thinking. "Something's not right here . . . Candrey!" he said aloud. "Jesse, you run and get Clements. Hurry!"

Malone didn't wait for Jesse's response, sprinting towards the back of the diner. The door was open and he slipped inside. The hair on his neck stood on end as he expected to catch a bullet at any time. Every muscle was taut . . . things had been too easy. He felt like a rat, just before the trap snaps shut. But Kell had no choice. If Candrey was in there with Rachel, she would need his help.

As he stepped into the kitchen with his guns drawn, he saw the cook and the waitress bound to a couple of chairs. Malone pulled a knife and quickly sliced the ropes from their wrists.

"She is inside, Senor Malone," Paco said. "Stadler and Yance wait for you there."

"Okay, Paco. Take the woman and get out the back door. Go now!"

"Gracias, Senor Malone. May God be with you."

"I hope so," Malone said.

For several minutes, he stood outside the kitchen door listening. No voices could be heard inside. No movement. Nothing!

Drawing his right hand gun, he pushed the door open slowly, with his other hand. Taking a deep breath, he stepped inside.

"We've been waiting for you, Mr. Malone. Holster your gun," said Candrey. "Don't worry about the woman. No harm has come to her . . . not yet."

Candrey spoke proudly, like a man convinced he had the upper hand. Nothing Kell saw convinced him otherwise. Rachel sat quietly in her chair, doing her best to remain calm. But the fear in her eyes gave her away. Next to her, holding a six-gun, there stood Yance Candrey. When their eyes met, he gave Malone an evil smile.

"When Mr. Hodges was late in returning, I had a feeling you must have killed him. Well done, Malone! I didn't think you could take him."

"Sorry to disappoint you, Candrey, but it wasn't me. Clements was the new law in Redhawk. He tried to arrest Montana, but Hodges would have no part of it."

The gunman turned lawyer shook his head. "I must have underestimated the man."

"A lot of folks did."

Rachel and Kell were in a tough spot. In order to come out on top, Malone knew he would need a cool head and a lot of luck. He was glad he favored a two-gun rig. Forced to go up against the likes of Tom Candrey, he would need every edge.

"You've been pulling a lot of strings since you first came to town, haven't you, Candrey?"

He smiled. "Adkins was a fool! Men who are hungry for wealth and power are men who can be used, manipulated for one's own needs. That's what I did with Clay."

"And Hodges?"

"He was just a pawn. When I was finished with him, he would have been expendable also. Skull Clements just saved me the trouble."

The man was cautious and deadly as a rattler. He always kept his gunhand free and ready. In a move designed to taunt him, the lawyer walked over behind Rachel, putting both hands on her shoulders. Behind her as he was, Kell could do nothing.

"But that brings me to what we should do with you and the woman, Malone."

"Let her go," Kell said. "She's got no part in this. You only wanted her to get to me."

"But you're wrong, Kellen Malone. Rachel is certainly not without her charms." She tried to pull away as he touched her. "I've always had a weakness for beautiful women."

Candrey walked away from Rachel, but Yance's gun still covered her.

"I asked her to be my wife, but she refused. No matter! After my needs have been satisfied, perhaps I will turn her over to my cousin. He appreciates a beautiful woman, also. He's been getting impatient."

Kell could see the gunman was growing weary of toying with them. Whatever happened would have to be soon.

"I've got other business waiting for me, Malone, business that calls for your disposal."

Something rattled outside the front door.

"Don't you go away, sweetie," Yance said, stroking her leg with his hand. He walked over, pulled back the shade, and peered outside. "I don't see anything, Tom. I'd better go have me a look."

Yance's exit would leave no one covering Rachel with a gun. Malone saw this as the break he was seeking.

As Tom's cousin opened the door, Jesse squeezed the shotgun's triggers. Both barrels hit the man at once, blasting him out of existence. The recoil knocked Jesse backward. The buckshot slammed Yance back through the doorway, his chest blown away.

At the first sound of gunfire, Rachel dived to the floor. With the woman free from the line of fire, Kell went for his guns . . .

As Candrey drew, Malone knew the man's reputation had been justly earned. The gun sprang to his hand in an instant, the fastest draw Kell had ever seen. Then both men were firing.

Candrey's gun drew first blood. One of the shots burned Kell's arm, only inches from his heart. Something then hit him low and hard. Kell gritted his teeth, dug in his heels, and returned fire. Both guns bucked in his hands, fast as he could work the triggers.

The diner roared with the explosions of gunfire. Smoke filled the air, the smell of powder burning his eyes. Malone squinted against the smoke and fought on.

His first two shots scored, hitting the outlaw in the chest and the neck. One of the others knocked the coffee pot from the table. Then Kell's guns hit him again and again. Candrey kept coming, cursing as he fired. The slugs tore at Malone's sleeves and hat.

The lawyer's white shirt had now blossomed into crimson. His gun was empty, but he kept advancing forward, the firing pin falling on empty chambers. The man was a walking corpse, driven by a fierce hatred and desire to kill.

Kell stepped aside and Candrey continued walking, stumbling over his cousin's lifeless body. He pitched over on his face. The lawyer then tried to stand, but his knees buckled under him. His body shook violently for a time and then stopped, the gun still clenched firmly in his hand.

Hesitantly, Jesse stepped into the doorway, hand on the trigger. He had already reloaded and was ready for further trouble. "Are you okay, Pa," he shouted.

"Yes, I'm fine, son" Kell answered, checking to make sure both outlaws were finally dead. Satisfied, he holstered his guns. "I'm glad you didn't listen to me. Don't know what I'd have done without your help."

Malone helped Rachel to her feet and she embraced him harder than he ever thought possible. "I was so scared! All I could think of was losing you, Kell!"

Malone smiled. "Looks like you're stuck with me now."

"That won't be so bad," she said, kissing him as their lips melted together.

Joe Clements and Buck Halstead came charging down the street, followed by several of the townspeople.

"Looks like we're too late," Joe grinned.

"Wasn't anything Jesse and I couldn't handle. Right, son?"

Proudly, the boy nodded.

Halstead swelled up like an overfed grizzly bear. "That boy's my nephew, Joe. He comes from mighty good stock!"

"That he does, Buck."

"Will you quit fussing over that little wound, Rachel?" Kell asked. "It will be fine."

"I saw you get hit, Kell. I still don't know how you kept from being killed."

Reaching into his vest pocket, Kell came out with his watch, twisted and scarred from Candrey's slug. "He came mighty close," Malone said with a laugh, holding it up for everyone to see. "That watch sent me to prison once. Cost me seven years of my life."

"Now it saved your life," Rachel added.

"Darned thing never did keep good time." Malone winked at Rachel and drew her into his arms. "By the way, Rachel, do you still have that wedding dress?"

"Why, Kellen Malone, if that's a marriage proposal, then my answer is yes. But you just got out of prison! I hope you didn't get too used to your freedom."

Coming Soon!

R.G. YOHO
DEATH RIDES THE RAIL
A KELLEN MALONE WESTERN
BOOK 2

Long before the advent of the U.S. Secret Service, Kellen Malone is called upon by the President of the United States to protect him from a ruthless and determined group of assassins, hell-bent on his destruction. Malone and Joe Clements team up as they ride the transcontinental railroad across the Old West, putting themselves in harm's way at every stop.

For more information
visit: www.SpeakingVolumes.us

On Sale Now!

MARK WARREN
AWARD WINNING AUTHOR

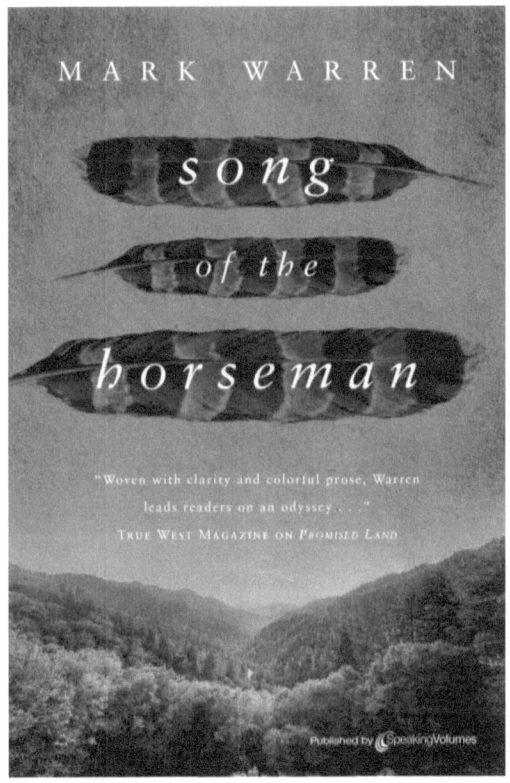

For more information
visit: www.SpeakingVolumes.us

www.ingramcontent.com/pod-product-compliance
Lightning Source LLC
Chambersburg PA
CBHW050518260626
47157CB00004B/1374